Caias Ward is a professional writer, editor, and game designer based in New Jersey, and has drawn from events in his own life to tell the poignant story of *The Only Brother*.

The Only Brother

Brother

CAIAS WARD

SADDLEBACK
EDUCATIONAL PUBLISHING

CUTTING EDGE

Breaking Dawn
DONNA SHELTON

The Finer Points of Becoming Machine
EMILY ANDREWS

Marty's Diary
FRANCES CROSS

The Only Brother
CAIAS WARD

The Questions Within
TERESA SCHAEFFER

Seeing Red
PETER LANCETT

© Ransom Publishing Ltd. 2008

This edition is published by arrangement with Ransom Publishing Ltd.

SADDLEBACK
EDUCATIONAL PUBLISHING
www.sdlback.com

ISBN-13: 978-1-61651-763-2
ISBN-10: 1-61651-763-8

Printed in Guangzhou, China
1111/CA21101799

16 15 14 13 12   1 2 3 4 5 6

To Ted, and his Million Lumen Life
February 2, 1969–February 2, 2006

CHAPTER 1

A gap in the family portrait

It's the quietest I'd seen him in a long time. Granted, the last time I *had* seen him was six weeks ago, at my birthday, and he was certainly loud then. His last words were, as always, criticizing something I was doing rather than being happy and encouraging. So I just walked out. Walked out on my own birthday. When I came back, he had gone home to New York; so that was the last time I talked to him.

And the worst part of it was that the parentals yelled at me for leaving, rather than him for mouthing off at me. "You should lighten up." "You need to relax."

It was my damn birthday, I shouldn't have my brother slamming me for everything I do and everything I am.

I looked down at him in the hospital bed. Two blood flow tests, they said, and they'd determined that William Simmons was brain dead. The parentals talked with doctors and nurses about organ donation and other arrangements. I just stared at the body and tried to say something.

"Didn't really hate you," I pushed out. "Just hated that everything *I* did well was expected and everything *you* did was rewarded."

His hand was still warm; his chest moved up and down with the help of a respirator. William was calm, peaceful. He wasn't complaining about medical problems, wasn't struggling with everything, wasn't angry at me and angry at the world.

William was brain dead. Two blood flow tests, reaction tests... and nothing there.

There was someone at the door.

"Andrew? You there, boss?" It was a heavy Jersey accent; tough and thick but still with a friendly tone. It sounded just like the people on MTV's "Jersey Shore."

It had to be Buzz. He was the only Chinese guy with a Jersey accent my brother knew. It's what happens when you go to college in New Jersey; strange things happen, like becoming best friends with a former Buddhist monk turned Philadelphia nightclub bouncer.

"Hey," I said.

Buzz stepped into the room, but not too close to me. Maybe my brother had told him about my personal space issues, maybe he could just read it. When my brother wasn't yelling at me or telling me I was screwing up, Buzz was a big part of the conversations we'd had.

"Namaste," he said, putting his hands together in front of his chest and bowing forward a bit. "I wish we could have met under better circumstances."

"So do I," I tried to smile. "Will made you sound like a superhero."

Buzz smiled. It was wide and bright. "Your brother really cared about you, you know?"

"I didn't know," I said.

Buzz pulled his head back a bit.

"He never said a word like that to my face," I said. "Never acted like he cared, either."

And then I waited for the arguments; "Of course he cared about you, he was your brother!" "You're just upset." "How can you say that?" Buzz didn't say any of those things though.

"I'm sorry he didn't find the words to express it in a way that you would understand," Buzz said.

That's new...

"Your parents are going to be busy, between forms and spending time in the chapel," Buzz continued. "They asked me to drive you back home whenever you are ready. I'll be outside the room; just let me know when you want to leave." He turned to walk out of the room.

"Buzz!" I said, a little louder than I should have.

"Yes?"

"Don't you... don't you want to say good-bye to him?" I whispered.

Buzz sighed, looking over at my brother... my brother's body. He touched his own head with his right hand, and then brought his hand to his heart.

"In some ways, he's not gone," he said. "And the others, we'll work around. Take your time, and do what you have to do. I'll be outside."

Buzz hadn't really looked at my brother the whole time he was in the room. It was creepy, in a way; it was like my brother was just furniture to him, like the bed or the table or the lamp. Great friends, college roommates, and fraternity brothers and... well, he wasn't freaking out or crying or even looking at him.

Buzz nodded to me, looked over at my brother, and stepped out of the room. He avoided a nurse as he moved a bit further down the hallway.

Confusing... just like everything. How the hell does my brother get through all the medical problems he had since birth, the recent brain surgeries, the recovery... and then go to a hospital for a pulled muscle and not come out? How do you dodge every bullet fired at you, recover, heal and go on with your life, and then get the plug pulled on you? How do you go from being a rising star lighting tech on Broadway to... to here, in a bed, on a respirator?

All I remember is the pain shooting through my hand, my knuckles bruised. I was in Buzz's rented car, loaded up with chips and a Coke and with an ice pack from the hospital on my hand.

"Hell of a punch," Buzz said as he drove. "Right through the drywall and nearly into the other side."

What the hell is wrong with this guy? I thought. The parentals freaked out, nurses swarmed me, and he's making light of it?

I shot him a look. He seemed to understand and changed the subject.

"I can either get upset about what happened to William," Buzz said, "Or I can remember all the great stuff. I can't control what happened to him. I can control how I react, though."

"You miss him?"

"Yeah," Buzz whispered. "Always kept in touch with him, as much as I could. Didn't expect last spring to be my last visit with him though. That was his first show on Broadway..."

Yeah, William was damn proud of that, his first lead lighting technician job. Parents dug deep for opening night tickets, front row, even with all my brother's bills for the surgeries. He could have got them tickets, but they insisted on front row and "no expenses spared!" while at the same time we were choking on the loan payments for the medical bills. Even I went, and I hated going to Will's stuff. Theater never interested me, and I was sick of how "wonderful" everything Will did was, how great he was doing, how incredible...

"Incredible show," Buzz interrupted my thoughts. "Something to be totally proud of."

"I guess." I kept the ice pack on my hand, turning it from one side to the other. It kept the swelling down, even as I flexed my fingers. Stupid move on my part, putting my hand into a wall. Hard to hold a stylus and tablet with a busted up hand, and I had paying graphics work coming up that week.

The ride took another hour of relative quiet before we finally pulled up to my road at about three in the morning. Buzz parked on the street in front of the house, moving the car after he almost parked next to a hydrant. It was my small chance to laugh as I pointed out the big driveway next to the big house where we lived. Buzz shrugged and pulled in. My hands were still full, so he helped me out of the car. He shuffled to the trunk, drained and worn out, the first time I'd noticed him really tired in the hours since we'd met.

"Yay, jetlag," Buzz said, shouldering his bag. "I need to get some sleep. Just point me to your guest room..." He smiled weakly, looking like he was about to fall over at any moment.

"Sure," I said, opening the door. He'd been traveling ten hours—his flight from Los Angeles to Chicago, then Chicago to New York, then he'd gone straight to Mt.

Sinai. Then the two-hour drive here after an hour at the hospital, and all for my brother.

"To the right, up the stairs, second door on the right. There's WiFi if you need it, just turn on your laptop. You have a surge protector?"

"Yeah, I do, don't want to blow out the computer. And I'd better let my wife know I'm okay," Buzz said as he shuffled up the stairs. He stopped halfway up and looked down at me.

"You want to talk, let me know. Otherwise, I'll let you be, okay?"

I tried to say something, but really couldn't think of much except "okay." He nodded at me and turned to go into the room.

I fell into my bed, checking my phone. Sara hadn't messaged me back. She'd said she was going camping that week; she might not have taken her phone with her.

When Sara drops off the face of the earth, she drops off the face of the earth...

Damn.

I sent her another text and just lay in bed with the ice pack on my hand. The hand was cold and red and hurt a lot. All the same, I wanted to keep on punching things. Just keep on punching things, even if my hand broke a dozen times.

CHAPTER 2

The next few days

Blog Entry For: Andrew Simmons
Mood: Pissed Off
April 9, 4:43 a.m.

William Simmons
April 9 1982 — April 9 2006

Ever forward...

Leave it to my brother to be late for his own departure. He's an organ donor so they are doing that stuff tomorrow; because of this, his body is still alive as of this moment even though his mind's, well, gone. And he managed to leave parting gifts; he'd just bought the family a laptop.

Blog Entry For: Andrew Simmons
Mood: Angry
April 10, 8:32 a.m.

Viewing for William Simmons:
Tuesday, April 11, 7—9 p.m.

Funeral of William Simmons:
Wednesday, April 12, 2—4 p.m.
Phillip & Sons Funeral Home
Old Cemetery Chapel Lane,
Westchester, NY

If you are someone who knows me well, show up if you want. If you are someone I only know in passing, best to e-mail me to see if it's okay.

Ever forward.

Blog Entry For: Andrew Simmons
Mood: Angry
April 12, 4:21 p.m.

So the guy who fixes my computer shows up to express his condolences. He and his father. They both own and work in the shop.

The Only Brother

My friends? The majority of them didn't even return e-mails or phone calls regarding it.

At least one gave a decent reason why he wasn't going to show up: "I never met your brother, I would be kinda uncomfortable seeing him for the first time in a box." Trevor.

Others had to work or wouldn't cut school. Some people e-mailed or responded to IMs. Most others didn't even return phone calls or e-mails. Still can't get in touch with Sara, she's still off in the wild Yorkshire Moors. She's going to flip when she finds out what happened; I know she'll be upset about not being around.

Anyway, the funeral was this afternoon. Am I the only person who doesn't like to be touched at funerals? Or in general? Seems so, because I literally had to shove people away as they tried to grab me. My Aunt Liza tried to hug me, I pulled away. Then Uncle James got mad at me. I almost busted up my hand again, especially when he mouthed off about that "damn fag goth makeup" I was wearing.

Buzz got between us and took me off to the side. Then he dragged that fatass and her husband to the back and said something to them, I don't know what exactly. All I know is that they just stayed shut up for the whole rest of the time. It's like he'd ended up yanking out their tongues. They wouldn't even say anything to the parentals. Like they were embarrassed or something...

And my name isn't Drew or Andy. It's Andrew. My father told all of them that, and they still insist on calling me Andy or Drew! Worst part is that when I try to be nice and say "could you call me Andrew?" they either get mad or go, "You'll always be Andy to me."

Well, you'll always be a fat bitch to me, Aunt Liza. Only reason your husband married you is because he knocked you up and you begged him to...

Mom and Dad's phones kept on ringing at the funeral home. Dad postponed his trip to Montreal for the director's meeting and the product release, but they kept on calling and calling... Mom had four property deals, two of them in Manhattan. Lord knows we need the money, so she had to keep everyone happy through the tears and my father speaking in French. One thing my brother left behind was a pile of medical bills. It's what happens when you want the best, like Beth Israel instead of the free clinic.

Drove with Buzz from the funeral home to church, walked into a church for the first time in about two years, sat in the back. One good thing about the parentals is that they never forced me to go to church. Figured that as long as I led a decent life and didn't hurt people, that was fine by them. Everyone was crying except me. I just didn't feel it. Just didn't feel anything.

At least Mom and Dad remembered to shut their phones off before they came into the church.

The parentals wanted me to ride to the cemetery with them, but I left them with my mom's sister and her husband. Buzz knew when to keep his mouth shut and not ask me things all the time. We left for the cemetery. I made Buzz stop so that I could get a Coke, got to the cemetery just after everyone else got there. They did the graveside thing, and everyone kept on crying. Buzz and I watched them lower the casket into the ground. Took a flower or two for some purpose. Went to the wake. Ate. Then went home.

School tomorrow. I would have gone the other days except I came down with this terrible cold. I went in on Tuesday and had to leave after three hours because I couldn't keep my head upright. They were shocked I even showed up, but you don't get an A if you don't show up and grind away.

And now, whatever else needs to happen. Stuff to clean, will to probate, estate to settle.

Ever forward.

Dear Sara,

I hope this letter finds you well. I'm sending it overnight so that it should arrive by the time you get back from your trip. As always, I hope you had fun wandering around in the moors. I never understood your fascination with nature, but I guess it's one of the things that makes you so special: a new surprise every time I think I know you.

I miss you very much, my friend. Since the last time I held you, many things have happened, many things have changed. It was a pure accident that you ended up in my class as an exchange student, yet you're one of the best things in my life. I wanted to get on that plane with you, get into your bed with you and not get out. Just lie in bed, wrapped around you, talking and laughing and being... being alive.

You'll probably find a bunch of texts on your phone, but I'll try to explain it with more sense here: my brother died while you were camping. He went into a coma after going to the hospital for a pulled muscle. Doctors did an autopsy, but we won't have the results for weeks. We thought he was through all these medical problems: the brain surgeries, the holidays in the hospital, the medications... We thought it was all over and he was going to go on with his life. But then he goes and dies.

And the worst part is, his last words to me were basically telling me to go to hell. I got some freelance work—great stuff for a graphics portfolio—and he had to criticize everything about it: who I was working for, what I was charging—everything. I just had to get up and walk out and wait for him to go back to New York and his big flashing lights. Walk out of my own home, just to avoid another fight where the parentals take his side again.

And six weeks later he's dead.

I blogged about the funeral, but I can fill in gaps. Buzz, Will's friend, is probably the only person who hasn't, as you put it, been a "wanker" to me. I'm not much for talking to anyone, but at least he knows this. He doesn't tell me how I should feel about my brother, or assume that I'll miss him, or that

I'm broken up about all this. He listened when I wanted to talk, talked when I didn't have anything to say, and let me know he was around if I needed anything.

I'm not broken up about my brother. I lost out on so many things because of him. He got full tuition to Rider, a private university in New Jersey, the full five years worth. Meanwhile, I'm working, laying out vinyl signs and doing freelance stuff and hope I have enough to pay for school. Seems some of my tuition money got spent on my brother's medical bills... so I have to make up the difference myself.

And every time I do something great, it's just like it's expected. Straight As? "We were certain you would get them." Even selling a piece of art at age twelve didn't get more than a shrug from the parentals. My brother ended up barely getting through school and they ended up showering him with gifts. I'm lucky the parentals put in the high speed internet I needed to sell the T-shirts I make. I have to keep most of that money hidden; they'll probably want me to pay for the damn funeral.

Jesus Christ, I didn't make him sick! I didn't screw up his delivery at birth, or give him nerve damage from the forceps squeezing his head, or mess up his life! I shouldn't have to pick up the damn pieces for him... I shouldn't have to give up the good stuff in my life so that he can have everything.

Not my damn fault.

I'll try to keep this short; I always feel bad about bringing this stuff up to you, complaining about things when I know you have your own problems. Find enclosed a few flowers from my brother's graveside. It may seem odd, but I figure that something as beautiful as these shouldn't just stand for death. Dry them out and use them as a reminder that even in bad times we can find beauty and hope.

You are those things to me. I will talk to you soon, my friend and love.

Love and Trust, Andrew.

The Only Brother

Blog Entry For: Andrew Simmons
Mood: Confused
April 14, 5:36 p.m., Protected Entry

Should I be crying?

My mother thinks I should. My father thinks I should.

At least the crazy New Jersey Buddhist doesn't. He says "grief is a personal thing" and I should express it the way I feel is right.

I had to fight the urge to dance on my brother's grave.

I shouldn't have to suffer for my brother's screwed-up life. I hated him then, I hate him now. He screwed up everything. There's always money problems now, medical bills, funeral bills, my parents fighting over gasoline costs, of all things. How the hell am I going to get to England for school if there isn't any money? How am I supposed to get away from here?

Still haven't heard back from Sara yet.

I don't want to be here anymore. I just wish it would end.

I love you Sara.

CHAPTER 3

Across the pond

GraphicAndrew: you there?

HaveYouSeenMyPants: OMG ANDREW!!! *TACKLEHUGPOUNCELOVE*

HaveYouSeenMyPants: I'm so sorry!!!! I just got your texts, I didn't even think to leave my phone on. I'm gonna call

GraphicAndrew: It's OK; don't feel like talking on the phone. My voice is ragged from fighting with the parentals

GraphicAndrew: *brings a sofa over*

HaveYouSeenMyPants: *sits all ladylike*

GraphicAndrew: *pounces*

HaveYouSeenMyPants: mmmmmmmmmm…

HaveYouSeenMyPants: you sure you don't want to talk?

GraphicAndrew: It's OK. Mom has taken to trying to overhear everything I say. This is the only way I know she's not listening

HaveYouSeenMyPants: I'm so sorry about your brother *hug* I wish I was there to help

GraphicAndrew: I wish you were here too. Just want to lie in bed and do nothing at all

HaveYouSeenMyPants: do nothing? ;)

GraphicAndrew: you are terrible

HaveYouSeenMyPants: I'm very good, from what you told me *lick*

GraphicAndrew: hehehe

GraphicAndrew: so how's your boy?

The Only Brother

HaveYouSeenMyPants: ☹

GraphicAndrew: that bad?

HaveYouSeenMyPants: we broke up

GraphicAndrew: I'm sorry

HaveYouSeenMyPants: just wasn't going to work. He kept on trying to change me, telling me all these things I could "fix" about myself. I'm perfectly fine, thankyouverymuch...

GraphicAndrew: well, there are a few things...

HaveYouSeenMyPants: HEY!!!

GraphicAndrew: jk

GraphicAndrew: just trying to find something to joke about, that's all

HaveYouSeenMyPants: I know

HaveYouSeenMyPants: so what can I do for you today?

GraphicAndrew: *sprawls out* just don't get it

HaveYouSeenMyPants: get what? *sprawls out with you*

GraphicAndrew: why he's such a damn saint to them

HaveYouSeenMyPants: *hug*

GraphicAndrew: I mean, I'm the one with the awesome grades, and making money with my art... and my brother's the one everyone looks to. All the damn time

HaveYouSeenMyPants: maybe they thought that he needed them more?

GraphicAndrew: so they just go and ignore the stuff I do?

HaveYouSeenMyPants: I don't know, love. I don't think they hate you. I mean, they didn't seem that way when I met them. They probably don't understand a lot of what you do

GraphicAndrew: I paint and draw. What's there to understand?

HaveYouSeenMyPants: Your dad's sold his soul to some big corporation and your mom's a realtor for the rich and famous. They make three times as much money as most of the people my parents know, and it's what they use to measure success: promotions, real estate deals, big vacations…

GraphicAndrew: yeah...

HaveYouSeenMyPants: so when they get a son who starts off in a blue-collar job, like lighting tech work, but uses it to move ahead, that makes sense to them. Your brother shows up to a job, collects a paycheck, that makes sense

HaveYouSeenMyPants: and with all his medical problems, especially with his birth, it was a lot harder for him to do things

GraphicAndrew: well, yeah. Damn doctor decides he wants to go on vacation on time, so he pulled my brother out with forceps.

Induced birth. It pinched a nerve and that messed up his motor skills

HaveYouSeenMyPants: the whole "thinking faster than he can act" thing?

GraphicAndrew: yeah. They put him in special ed classes until my mother made them test him without the stupid time limits. Then they found out he was a genius. He did great in school, once they realized he had a disability. It's how he got into that theater school in New Jersey

HaveYouSeenMyPants: yeah, the one about an hour away from the city

GraphicAndrew: and my parents poured every cent they could into him going there, because he "overcame so much" and it's "his dream" and "blah blah blah." And he has to take a year off for yet more surgery

HaveYouSeenMyPants: for the swelling at his brain stem?

GraphicAndrew: yeah. They thought he was in the clear after his delivery, but twenty years

later more stuff comes up. And then he ate
his way through a year of school, so he had
to spend another year in school when he
almost flunked out. All at my parents' expense.
Meanwhile, I have to account for every damn
buck I spend on anything, and they expect me
to work just to help pay his bills and they never
say a damn thing about anything good I do!!!

HaveYouSeenMyPants: *hug*

GraphicAndrew: why the hell is everything
I do "expected" but every lame thing he did
rewarded? I have dreams too! I've been
selling shirts with my designs, and taking
commissions and putting it all away so that I
can get the hell out of here. Put a damn ocean
between me and them and never look back. I
didn't try to get in his way, but that's how they
saw it. It was either Will or me for everything...
and Will won, every time

HaveYouSeenMyPants: I wish there was
more I could do to help

GraphicAndrew: it's OK. I just don't want to
be here any more

HaveYouSeenMyPants: *hug* don't say that, please...

GraphicAndrew: he's a saint, he can do no wrong no matter what happens. And I'm just trouble, and "selfish," and...

HaveYouSeenMyPants: you are not selfish! You do more for people than anyone I know. You even help people you barely know!

GraphicAndrew: I'm going to go

HaveYouSeenMyPants: no...

HaveYouSeenMyPants: please don't go

> **GraphicAndrew is offline**

HaveYouSeenMyPants: DAMMIT, ANDREW!!!!

HaveYouSeenMyPants: if you come back, just be OK... *hug*

The Only Brother

Whatever you do, just promise me
you're OK, OK?

Please let me know you're OK? *hug*
And don't do anything that will hurt you.

I'm OK for now. Thanks. Trust you.

Trust you too. I'm glad you're OK. Just
call me when you need to, OK?

I will.

CHAPTER 4
Sorting a life

We turned Will's old room into a staging area for all his stuff. There was so much of it, Dad and I made six trips with the minivan from the city to here. Six long, drawn out, agonizing trips where Dad would do nothing but alternate between talking in French to IT guys and project leaders, and going on and on to me about all the "fun times" we had on vacation.

It's been four months since the funeral. They still keep talking about him, over and over, all the time. It's all "Will would have laughed at that" or "that was Will's favorite program" or "the cheese in that omelet looks like Will." They see Will in clouds, just like those old bats seeing Jesus in a water stain on trees outside their houses. If they weren't so private, the parentals, they would gather up all the family to sit and stare at this sort of crap for hours.

The last vacation, by the way, wasn't that much fun. Mostly it was fighting with Will because I wasn't clumsy or because I wasn't sick all the time or because I didn't have a funny-shaped head. Yes, Will had a funny-shaped head, and he was all those other things that happen when the doctor induces the pregnancy and pulls you out with forceps, all because he doesn't want to miss a day of his own damn vacation. Pinched a nerve on my brother, which resulted in all these problems he had: clumsy motor skills, his mind literally working faster than he could express himself and the frustration that comes with all of that.

"I miss Spain," my dad said, pulling back into the inside lane. "Will loved it. Just lying out on the beach, swimming... I wish you had come out more the last time. I swear you chained yourself to that computer of yours."

"It was a nice villa," I said, not even looking up from my sketch. "Why would I want to leave? Besides, I did go out and do lots of stuff."

"Yes, by yourself, sketching the place like it was going to disappear. Who brings a suitcase full of paper and pens on vacation? You should have been out having fun!"

He put his hand on my shoulder and shook me. Fortunately, I'd pulled my pencil away from the paper.

Who brings a suitcase full of paper and pens on vacation? The artist who is walking around a place that dates back over a thousand years with some of the most amazing architecture you will ever see. Besides, the best way for any boy to meet a girl out in the world is to make it look like you are starting to sketch her. I keep a few starts of sketches in my papers so that if I see a girl I like, I can start some work on it and when she notices me, it looks natural. Sara thought this was positively awful, but admitted it had worked on her.

Sure I was out having fun, what with sketching girls and buildings and the apes in Gibraltar. It's not every day you get to draw animals in the wild on a mini excursion. They just never noticed.

"We were very lucky to get that place," Dad rambled on. "It's one of the advantages of the job, all these rich people with no time to enjoy the things they buy themselves. Not that we're badly off ourselves, all things considered. Just not "super-rich" yet," he took his hands off the steering wheel to make air quotes. He'd seen it in a movie and thought it made him look cool. I'll let him have that one, if it gives me a moment's peace.

It's amazing what you can draw from memory if it's a strong enough one. Family, friends, dreams, hopes... Sara. It was some silly photo Sara and I took, she gave me rabbit ears above my head without telling me. I had no clue what she was doing, even after one of my friends took the shot. I rotate the picture as the desktop background for my computer and on my phone, but it's not like I even need the picture to remember that moment.

Sara and I were at my friend Trevor's, watching TV, and just balled up on the sofa together. Everyone else was drinking and smoking and whatever, about a dozen of us all over in Trevor's basement. His parentals were never around and never actually took stock of the liquor cabinet, so everything flowed freely. Sara and I weren't ones to drink or smoke, or anything; just not our thing. You could say that our vice was each other. I couldn't get enough of her and she couldn't get enough of me.

It wasn't even the sex—although there was lots of sex. No, it was just having someone there you could talk to, laugh with, be around without any pressure. Someone just accepting who you are, no matter how strange you turn out to be.

"I'm your friend, dammit," she would yell at me, "which means you aren't ever going to get rid of me, even if I have to strap you to the hood of my car!"

No hang-ups about who likes who, or who's going to be serious about what, or anything. Just two people spending time with each other and not caring what anyone thought of it.

Classes flew by with her, days and nights stood still, and a year of study was just moments. It was everything I ever saw in those afternoon movies I usually changed the channel from, but she insisted we keep on watching. Yet it wasn't like she was a girlfriend; just a friend who I trusted with lots of thoughts concerning my life. A friend who happened to be a girl.

And Trevor takes pics of everyone. Good pics, like the boob shot of Emma when she bent over to pick something up, and bad pics like Bobby passed out and Ricky sticking his ass in Bobby's face. But then there was our shot, Sara and I just tangled up in each other watching the TV and talking about which *Star Trek* is the best one—

And then a gray scar of pencil mark scrawled across Sara's face as my dad slapped my shoulder and kept his hand there. It ran from jaw to forehead on her, almost ripping the paper.

"Jesus Christ!"

"What?" my dad said, still keeping his hand on my shoulder.

"You messed up my drawing! What the hell is wrong with you?"

I took out one of my gum erasers, working on the scar with plastic surgeon skill. I could always fix it on the computer after I scanned it, but that's not the point. Once again, my parentals get in the way and screw up something I've worked on, something that was mine. They never did that to Will, never got in the way of anything he did.

"It was an accident."

"Just don't touch me, okay?" I hissed.

"All right." My dad sank into his seat, finally pulling his hand away.

I kept working on Sara's face, dabs and wipes and touches of the eraser finally restoring her to her natural tone of pencil shades.

"I just don't want anyone touching me," I mumbled to my dad.

"You never have, Andrew," he said. "I just don't get it, though. We're all that we've got now—you, me and your mom. And you keep on fighting us about everything." His voice trailed off, cold and hollow like it does when he tells anyone how he is doing *all right*.

"I'm not fighting anything. Just don't want you touching me." I kept on sketching, finally cleaning everything up.

"I swear, you've always been like this." His hands squeezed the wheel. "Never wanted anyone touching you as a baby, no hugs growing up." He laughed weakly. "Mom always thought you were a little grumpy old man in a baby's body. Never made a fuss as a baby..."

Not like you would have listened if I *had* said anything. Maybe I'd screamed up a storm and you didn't notice between driving Will to various doctors. Maybe I didn't go *look at me, look at me!* all the time, because I'd already figured you were doing all your looking at Will. Maybe I didn't want to waste my time. Maybe there were better things to do than fight for something I was never going to get.

And through all this, Dad just kept on talking at me. He was back to talking about Will, and all the wonderful things Will had done. His college degree and his work, and how he lost all this weight, and... well, so on, and so on. Fortunately, I only had to take another half-hour of this before we arrived at my brother's old apartment in Chelsea. Not bad, as far as places go: two bedrooms, an assortment of other small rooms and the remains of a mess we'd finally made a dent in over the past few months.

We could finally see the floor, with many things already boxed up and ready to go. My brother had paid a few months in advance so we had another month before we needed to get everything out of the apartment. It was my job to ship out everything my brother had sold on eBay before he died. All of that sat in my room—boxes and boxes of coins and books and whatever other junk Will sold off when he'd got bored with it. Hours of sending boxes out by mail, fighting with my parents to get the money back for the postage, fighting with people because their auctions were late. *Look, I didn't kill my brother just so that your auction would be late. I need your address again.*

At least Will kept records, so I could get into his accounts. For a rampant slob who once got a whole stick of butter into the top of his video cassette recorder, he was meticulous when it came to his auctions. Checks and PayPal transfers right into the trust account and right back out as fast as we could; no sense in his credit card debts eating up the money. And we had to pay the medical bills somehow...

"Andrew!"

"What?"

I guess I must have zoned out. I held a picture frame in my hand, polished steel. It was Will and me on Christmas morning, three years ago. We were just coming down from the top of the stairs and my dad decided he just had to take a picture. My brother was in his hat phase, covering the scars and his bald head from his— fifth?—round of surgery. Yeah, fifth brain operation, this time to take out a shunt that drained spinal fluid from the base of his brain stem into his stomach. Will's hat was silly, with a stuffed lobster sticking out of the front.

And me, bleary-eyed—I'd been up all night working on a picture—barely awake and barely able to stand after the flash went off in my face. My brother thought this was as funny as ever, just like Mom and Dad did. They always thought it was "fun" to take my picture when I didn't want it, to keep on touching me, to keep talking when I just wanted to work. I only ever talked when I had something to say.

"Andrew!"

Dad hovered over me, and I wasn't able to cover the picture in time. He put his hands on my shoulders and looked.

"That was a great Christmas," he said.

I don't get it. I just don't get it. How can he call that a great Christmas when William smacked me around, when I got screamed at for hitting him back, when my own brother called me a fag for drawing and for dressing how I wanted? I have no idea how he could think I'd call it "great" when Will just acted up, but they would insist that it was my fault every time something crappy happened...

"I guess," was the best I could push out of my mouth. I threw the picture into a box with piles of old clothing, putting it from my mind as best I could. All this would end up on eBay. I'd scan the pic at least, and save it. Every picture needed to be scanned now, all so that no one would ever forget William and his wondrous achievements.

More packing, more loading, more junk. I can't even imagine what the place looked like the first time Dad got here to get Will's suit for the funeral. Probably takeout containers as far as the eye could see, porn, and catalogs for theater lighting equipment. Dad stayed at the apartment overnight that time; probably cleaned the place up as much as he could, so Mom didn't have to see it all. She certainly wouldn't have been able to handle the porn.

Every once in a while, Dad stopped and stared at something: book, a shirt, a hat... something that reminded him of Will. I kept quiet; I didn't want to get sucked into the gloom. I know it hurts him a lot, but I didn't do it. I didn't kill Will, and I shouldn't always have his ghost haunting me.

Don't know how much I'll forget, though.

And then, Will's old room, stacked with boxes I hadn't had a chance to go through yet. It was easier when Mom was off selling homes. I could sneak out trash, keep the saleable stuff and put the pictures to the side.

I knew what really would mean memories to the parentals, what they could live without and what we could just throw away.

Mom, on the other hand, didn't have any idea what was worth saving and what was trash. She would have bought another house to keep everything. "No! It was his!" Like throwing anything out was like throwing away a precious memory.

Mom pulled at the painting. I let it go, not wanting to deal with the fallout if it ripped. It was finger paints on paper, ragged on one edge where Will tore it out of the big pad of paper. The head on the dog twisted impossibly off the black and gray stick figure body, blue ears and yellow teeth and not much else. Next to it stood a kennel, straight and tall with perfect angles and perspective, drawn in fine-lined ink. Under both pictures was Will's illegible scrawl of a signature, sloppy even for a seven-year-old boy.

Mom brushed it smooth, placing the painting carefully in a manila folder. This, she set aside, just like the sloppy fired clay pot, the sloppy tie-dye T-shirt Will made at a party as a kid, and the sloppy first draft of his college thesis written in four different colors of ink and stained with soy sauce. She didn't care where she set it aside, not even noticing that it was in the way. I had to sort all of this, and get all the stuff sold, but that didn't matter to her.

"Mom, we don't have the space for all of this..."

"Nonsense," Mom shushed me, "I'll find a spot. I always find a space for everything."

"What, so we can live in a storeroom? Mom, there's too much stuff to keep..."

Mom sat down slowly and rested her head in her hands. She shuddered and then cried, her head shaking. I stepped away, not sure what to do. At the funeral, I hadn't been able to get my head around the idea of hugging Mom, or holding her hand, or anything, really. Still can't do it now after these few months. It just doesn't feel right for me to do it. Like I said, I never really was a touchy-feely person.

I didn't even notice Dad in the doorway of the room. He moved quickly to Mom, wrapping his arms around her. She turned to him, holding on, shaking and sobbing.

Why couldn't I understand this? I just didn't feel the same way about them as they claimed to feel about me. I thought about hugging them, or saying I cared, but then realized that I couldn't say any of those things. How do you care about people who don't care back? How do you care about people who always had a favorite, and it wasn't you, not by a long shot? You don't. You go, and to places where you are wanted, to people who want you just as much as you want them.

Trevor was my ticket. He had a job and, more importantly, was old enough to drive. I gave him a quick ring, music blasting out of my phone when he picked up.

"Andrew!" Trevor's solid Hoosier accent

boomed from out of my phone, shaking my hand. Sara said it was like "an Irishman whispering."

"Quiet," I shushed him over the phone. "I need you to pick me up quick."

"I got a few in me, but I'm okay to drive I think. We're going to watch some football. Hope the Jets kick Dallas's ass!" I covered my phone again as I loaded my laptop and drawing tablet into one of my bags. I had so much work to do and wasn't getting any of it done.

"It's one in the afternoon on a Saturday, Trevor."

"Been drinking since ten. Like you said, it's a Saturday. What have you been doing?"

"Sorting through my brother's crap," I said.

"That's crap," Trevor bubbled. "You need to throw back a few, see some of the girls coming over, have some fun, like."

"I have work to do. Just need a power outlet."

"Fine, fine, be all responsible," Trevor said "responsible" like it would steal his beer money. "But at least you should come over. I'll be there in ten."

He hung up, just as loud as he talked. Trevor's not the brightest guy in the world, but he's fun and a good friend in a fight. Finally getting all my stuff together, I worked my way down the stairs as quietly as possible.

"Andrew!" my dad yelled from the room. "Where are you going?"

"Out!" I yelled back, not even stopping. I heard him thumping down the stairs after me.

"You can't go out," he said, "we have too much stuff to do here. Your mother has two closings this week, and I have to fly out to Montreal. We need you to go through all this stuff."

"I have a lot of work to do, Dad. Trevor's picking me up."

I stopped about one step from the bottom of the stairs, my father coming down fast. I backed my way down, wondering what my odds were of getting out without a fight.

"That Trevor is a terrible influence! Dammit, Andrew, you have responsibilities now! You know we are expecting you to carry through…"

Zero chance of getting out without a fight.

"Expecting? Expecting?" I screamed. "I've been doing everything left and right for years! I designed the prayer cards to save us some money! I stayed up late on school nights to get all that stuff listed on eBay so that we could pay my brother's bills! I barely have time to study! And yes, I *do* have to work to get good grades, it's not just a given!"

"Andrew, do not use that tone…"

"Every pay increase you got," I spat at him, "every commission Mom made, all went to paying Will's medical bills and his big college bill and his eating his way through a damn year of school because he was "sad!""

"Don't you ever talk to me like that!"

"My laptop, I earned! The tablet, I earned. I didn't get to study overseas because of Will's third operation! We spent three Christmases in a hospital where I got to hear everyone bitch about how I wasn't being "festive!" I didn't put him in there!"

And now Mom decides to cry her way into the argument. I couldn't understand her at first, but one word came out loud and clear.

"Selfish."

Yes, I'm so damn selfish, getting barely anything for holidays because my brother needed something. So selfish that when I offered to help my brother in his design classes because *I'm a damn artist and might know what I am doing*, he would still mouth off at me on the phone and in e-mails. So selfish that I had tried to help where I could, in the ways I could help best, but he and the parentals hadn't wanted any part of it.

"I'm out of here, I'll see you tomorrow." I made it to the door before a hand dug into my shoulder.

Next thing I saw, Dad was flat on his back on the stairs, his nose swollen and bloody. I don't even remember what happened, much. I must have given him a slap and done it right for once, since I didn't hurt my hand. I don't remember opening the front door, I don't remember running down the driveway...

But I was at the end of the drive in no time, running down the street in the direction I knew Trevor would have to come from his place. I caught him two streets early, throwing myself into his crappy Corolla with the dented side, and yelling at him to drive, drive, drive...

The Only Brother

Sitting in Trevor's car, I couldn't even focus on anything he was saying other than "like" and "like" and "like" in that nonstop way of his. The past two months kept on pushing back into my head, two months of fights and shrinks and my life going to hell...

CHAPTER 5

How does that make you feel?

Trevor was talking as he drove, the way he always does, nonstop. But my mind was back two months in the past. Creepy shrinks.

"So, how does that make you feel?"

Dr. Thompson looked at me with his bug eyes, peering out from behind thick glasses that he constantly cleaned with a blue cloth. He was friendly enough for an ancient guy, I guess. But I'm not one for doctors, especially ones who want to load me up with medications. And the ones he prescribed for me would make an elephant pass out. Still, it was good to talk to someone who didn't judge me, or everything that I did.

I considered his question for a moment. "Angry, I suppose."

I fidgeted in the chair. I always thought the crazy people were supposed to lay down on a couch when they talked to a shrink. But Thompson had directed me right to a big leather chair facing him. He warned me about my wallet chain scuffing the leather; I picked it up and brought it over my lap. It was about sixteen inches of comfort to fidget with in an uncomfortable place.

This guy had no sense of design: wood panelling, too much furniture in too small a room, three big leather chairs, a monstrous desk, a not-quite matching leather couch, and walls stuffed with bookshelves and diplomas.

Dr. Vernon Thompson, Class of '74. Harvard Medical School. Member in Good Standing of Blah Blah Blah Association.

I'd done my own checking on the guy. He wasn't a criminal or anything, had had some articles published. Dealt with adults mostly, but also *grief issues*, which is why my parentals had dumped me here once a week for the past two weeks.

The place even smelled old.

"Why do you feel angry?"

Because old people keep asking me stupid questions? How about my parents bitching at me over every little thing in the world? Oh, I know! What about getting outclassed by a damn ghost?

"Everyone keeps on asking me how I'm doing..."

"And how does that make you feel?" he asked again.

"Annoyed," I said. "I mean, almost everyone who asks already assumes they know the answer. About everything. At Will's wake, my Uncle Alan started going on about how "close" Will and I were. So I told him "well, no, we weren't." And he just shut up, didn't know what to say at all. One of my cousins who asked me how I was, basically called me a liar when I said I was fine. I told him to go to hell."

"Do you think this was the right thing to say?"

Well actually, yeah, sure I did. Uncle Alan saw my brother at holidays and picnics, so what did he know? *I* saw my brother when he came home drunk from a party, and vomited in my shirt drawer. Of course, this was after his first operation, so it was "okay" then. At least that's what my father said. As for my cousin, well, I'd been fine with him until he'd called me a liar. Again, what the hell did he know?

"I really don't care if it was right or not. I just said it."

I jangled the chain, counting links with my fingers as I watched Thompson exhale and wipe his glasses with that blue cloth.

Why is it always something that *I* did that was wrong? Didn't any of them think that what anyone else said could ever be the problem?

"I'm sure your uncle and cousin didn't mean to upset you, Andrew. They were grieving just like everyone else."

Not grieving like me. Nor hating. Or maybe just not loving or whatever the hell you could call it. Can't any of them see that I'm just... well, confused that I can't ever make anything between Will and me work now? I can't start over, or get him to see that he was wrong about lots of stuff. Can't get him not to bitch at me about how I look, or what I paint, or even just get him to go "hey, you actually know what you are doing." I can't ever make anything happen regarding my brother and the way he was with me. And all I'm left with is the memory that his last words to me were just more damn criticism.

"Andrew?"

"Huh?" I'd been lost in my own bitter thoughts.

"Did you hear what I said?"

"Oh, yeah," I said. "Sure."

"I think that you might need to be a bit more mindful of the things you say to others," the good doctor said. "Communication is a two-way street, and if you want to get better reactions from people you have to take that into account."

I shrugged at him. It was all ridiculous...

"How are your other relationships going?"

"All right, I guess. I have a few friends, and I get along fair enough with other people. I miss Sara a lot, though. The sex, yeah, but mostly I just miss someone who understands me and what's going on in my life."

"Have you tried to build more local relationships, Andrew?"

"Huh?" I said.

"What I mean is," the doctor said, "Have you tried to form associations with people near to you? Even just friendships? With people you can turn to?"

"Well, yeah," I said. "But with all the stuff concerning my brother, it's been hard to focus on anything."

"Why is that?"

"Parents wanting me around for anything, everything, means I could never really find the time to spend with my friends. Besides, with the money situation, I've had to work and the best way is doing design work, layouts and stuff, online. So I couldn't chill with anyone and I've kind of grown apart from people, and some haven't taken it that well."

"But you managed to fit Sara into your life?"

I shrugged. "Yeah, I could squeeze her in." With no parentals here except her host family, she could make the time for me. I kept up with Trevor, but he didn't give a damn if I disappeared for a week or a day; he was just around. But Sara, she didn't expect anything, especially what I couldn't give.

"I'm not a strong fan of this relationship," Dr. Thompson said. "It seems very distracting to the building of real relationships, that is to say, local ones."

Did he just say that my relationship with my best friend wasn't real?

"I understand your emotional attachment to her is strong," Dr. Thompson said. "But have you considered cutting back on the work you are doing and trying to resocialize with your other friends?"

"I'm not exactly the most popular guy with them right now."

"Why do you say that?" Thompson asked.

Um, because, because kids my age are

bitchy and turn on people in a second? You'd think he'd know that.

"I didn't have the time for them, so they took it personally."

"I do think," Thompson rubbed his glasses again, "you should consider focusing on other relationships. As always, some relationships fade in and out. Your friend Sara is very far away, so it might be best to focus on people near to you as well."

"So you want me to ditch my best friend?"

"I didn't say that. I just think you should find relationships that are closer to you."

All right, this is the last time I'm in this office.

"But our time is up this week," Thompson said, pointing to the ugly clock on his wall. "I'm going to keep you on the medication for another two weeks. Just let me know how they make you feel. Any reactions so far?"

"Yeah. My sex drive sucks and I can't focus."

"Hmm," he huffed. "We'll give it a few more weeks and work from there. Okay?" He smiled at me through his beard.

Yeah, right. Nice knowing you, grandpa.

GraphicAndrew: *falls over onto a sofa*

HaveYouSeenMyPants: that tired, love?

GraphicAndrew: just drained. Haven't been able to focus on anything lately

HaveYouSeenMyPants: *cuddles up with you*

HaveYouSeenMyPants: *bite*

GraphicAndrew: God, I can't even think of playing now...

HaveYouSeenMyPants: OK, where is Andrew and what have you done with him???

GraphicAndrew: :J

GraphicAndrew: just the new meds this doc has me on. Wiped out completely. And I don't trust him. I'm going to see if I can get a new doctor. He doesn't like you. :(

HaveYouSeenMyPants: screw him. He doesn't even know me. I'm sure that if he met me he wouldn't like me at all, but at least let him judge me face to face. :)

HaveYouSeenMyPants: so what did the witch doctor put you on?

GraphicAndrew: beta blockers for anxiety, lithium for my supposed mood swings, except my moods aren't swinging anywhere

HaveYouSeenMyPants: oh God...

GraphicAndrew: what?

HaveYouSeenMyPants: *hug*

GraphicAndrew: what?

HaveYouSeenMyPants: you need to get off the lithium. That stuff will turn you into a zombie!

GraphicAndrew: I've noticed. It sucks

HaveYouSeenMyPants: I told my parents to go to hell once I looked up what it did. I'll email you all the links I put together on it, in case yours fight you on it

GraphicAndrew: "in case?" Of course they are going to fight me on it

HaveYouSeenMyPants: just show them all the stuff and I'm sure they won't keep feeding you all those pills

GraphicAndrew: what about the beta blockers?

HaveYouSeenMyPants: they're alright. Just takes an edge off the panic attacks and the anger stuff. How are those going?

GraphicAndrew: a bit better. Don't feel so wired. I can actually get some work done

HaveYouSeenMyPants: that's good

GraphicAndrew: yeah

HaveYouSeenMyPants: *poke poke*

GraphicAndrew: hehehehe

HaveYouSeenMyPants: I miss you, you know that?

GraphicAndrew: yes

GraphicAndrew: yes I do. I miss you too

HaveYouSeenMyPants: you got more work?

GraphicAndrew: yeah, I'm working in a print shop. Mom insisted I get a "real" job instead of sitting at my computer all day

HaveYouSeenMyPants: :P

HaveYouSeenMyPants: jerks. You make 25 dollars an hour doing design work, and they want you to work behind a counter and get paid whatever the minimum wage is in your strange American money?

HaveYouSeenMyPants: :)

GraphicAndrew: my dad wanted me to work in a deli. I told him to go to hell

HaveYouSeenMyPants: I hated working in a deli

HaveYouSeenMyPants: btw, you gonna see that hot girl you went out with before I showed up? :) Did you find out if she's still sweating for you?

GraphicAndrew: :P

GraphicAndrew: you mean Caroline? That's not going to work out

HaveYouSeenMyPants: why not?

HaveYouSeenMyPants: if you don't want her, I'll take her ;)

GraphicAndrew: her crowd and my crowd just won't work. She's popular and I'm just weird

HaveYouSeenMyPants: :(

HaveYouSeenMyPants: that's a shame. You told me the sex was electric

GraphicAndrew: yeah... she's hot and all. And not dumb, just doesn't show off that she's smart

HaveYouSeenMyPants: she can't be that smart if she's not jumping you at every moment. I mean, I'd do you... again :)

GraphicAndrew: hehehehe

GraphicAndrew: I have to get to work. You want to call me later?

HaveYouSeenMyPants: not tonight, I'm going to be out. Tomorrow?

GraphicAndrew: I'll call around six tomorrow

HaveYouSeenMyPants: that will be midnight my time

GraphicAndrew: yes, it will. I will be stuck in the past while you are enjoying the future

GraphicAndrew: hahahahahahahaha

GraphicAndrew: </maniacal laughter>

HaveYouSeenMyPants: hehehe!

GraphicAndrew: love you

HaveYouSeenMyPants: love you too!

"So, how does that make you feel?"

New office, new psychiatrist, all in the two weeks since Dr. Thompson told me to ditch my best friend.

"Well, since I stopped taking the lithium," I said, "I actually feel *something*. Much better now. I can actually think about sex now. Sara's been bugging me about getting "back in the saddle," as she puts it, since phone sex and web cams only go so far and she wants me to be happy."

This office, at least, was warm, and inviting, and I actually felt okay coming here. The doc wasn't ancient, either. Younger than my dad, well dressed and well spoken. He wasn't a jerk about things, at least so far. I'd dumped Thompson and his always-dirty glasses after fighting with the parentals for an hour, and they'd found someone else on the list of *Doctors Who Help Crazy People*.

"It's really not a good idea to stop taking your medication, Andrew." The doctor—Berger—leaned forward in his seat, concerned. "There can be adverse reactions."

"What?" I said. "Like getting excited when I like a girl? I like the idea of everything working, believe it or not."

"We can make adjustments to the medication..."

"The only adjustment I want is for everything to work when I need it to work."

Berger laughed, nodding at me.

"We'll work on it. I still want you on the lithium, but we'll lower the dosage. How have you been getting along with your parents?"

"I haven't. I keep getting screamed at to get a job," I said. "I have a job. I make twenty-five dollars an hour just designing, not including the T-shirts I sell. But I found a sign shop that doesn't flip out on me for wearing what I do under the uniform shirt. At least the shirt goes with my pants." I tugged at my "Sign Time" black button-down shirt, matching the black of the shirt to my baggy wide-legged black jeans.

"So tell me more about your brother."

Wow, what a way to shift the conversation.

"He was a jerk."

Dr. Berger pulled his head back and took down some notes with his chrome pen. A lot of notes, scribbling away.

"What are you writing?" I asked.

"Just notes for me to refer back to," he said, looking up at me after he spoke. "Why do you think he was a jerk?"

"Just was," I said. "I mean, it's like every time there was a choice between him and me, it was always him. Everything I did, Mom and Dad just expected it to happen. Top grades in school, anchor on the track team, even my first paying design—it was like, "we expected that." My brother though? Everything was a miracle and they let him know it."

"He was really sick, right?"

"If you call getting your head scrunched with forceps and five brain operations "sick" then yeah," I said. "Sucked for him, and it's a shame it happened. But my parentals forgot that they had another son. Getting forgotten sucks a lot too. And *I* didn't make all that crap happen to my brother."

My hands hurt; I kept on digging my nails into my palms. I hated talking about this stuff. I didn't want to be here, but Dad said he'd take my computer if I didn't show up and try to "get better." So, I'm here. Maybe I can get something out of it.

"I don't think your parents forgot you," Berger said. "This is a lot for them to handle, from the operations to the funeral. Even when he was growing up, think of all the problems Will had with socializing. You didn't need as much from them, so it might seem that your parents didn't care as much."

"So I'm just the self-sufficient kid? I didn't actually need them to treat me like their son?"

"I'm not saying that," Berger said.

"But it's what you mean. Just because I didn't "need," like you claim, doesn't mean I didn't want or deserve. Add in all the times I did stuff and my brother got mad at me because I *could* do it and he still had trouble, even though he was ten years older than me. Was it my fault that I could fix things when I saw how they worked, once, or type seventy words a minute to his ten?"

"It is possible there were some jealousy issues," Berger said. "But you had so many advantages over your brother."

So much for this working out.

"So what is the best advantage?" I asked him.

"What?"

"Yeah, my best advantage," I asked. "What was it?"

"The best advantage?"

"Yes, what's the best advantage I had? Is it my brother trashing my toys when he'd get angry? Or my parentals deciding to spend our vacation money on my brother's weight loss surgery when he ate his way through his second year in his snobby private college in Jersey and put on 84 pounds? How about them making me feel like hell because *I* want to go away to college, like he did?"

I stood up and tucked my wallet chain away.

"The session isn't over yet, Andrew," Berger said

"How about the fact that I will never be able to match up to a dead twenty-six-year-old who beat the crap deal he'd been given, and didn't end up pumping gas or sweeping floors for a living? How's that for an advantage?"

I was out of the door before he could say anything. I wasn't going to listen anyway. He really wasn't listening to me, either.

———

Two weeks after Berger and his insistence on my "advantages," the school sent a letter to the house...

Dear Mr. & Mrs. Simmons,

I am writing to you with regard to your son, Andrew. Recently, his behavior in school has shown changes for the worse. He is constantly disrupting classes and arguing with both other students and his teachers. His grades have declined, even in his best classes, and there is a decided lack of effort in subjects where Andrew has previously shown great enthusiasm.

We would like to arrange a meeting with you both, so that we may discuss this matter and develop a solution together. We would also like to arrange an additional meeting, with Andrew present, where we can all agree on the course of action that we all feel will contribute to Andrew's advancement and success.

We understand the challenge that your family has faced regarding your son William and will support you in any way possible regarding Andrew's well-being and continued educational success. It is our hope that together we may effect a return to Andrew's earlier enthusiasm for his education, and a subsequent improvement in his grades to their previous levels.

Yours sincerely

Dr. Alice Hull

Dean of Students

I didn't pay much attention in the meeting, at least to what my parentals said. Dr. Hull, however, isn't the easiest person to fool. Besides, she actually wanted me to do better, and focused on me and how I felt. I played along with my parentals, nodding when I needed to, agreeing when I needed to, even throwing out a few ideas on how I could be a better student.

Of course, I *want* to be a better student. I figure four more AP classes will get me into any college I want, including overseas ones. I've been looking at Oxford and Cambridge in England, and a few others here. I can pull my grades up before the end of the semester, enough that they'll look good when I apply to schools. I may take a gap year, I may not. I have money put away in a savings account my nana set up for me when I was born; I've just kept on putting money into it and my parents don't even know it's there. I do my banking online, so there's never a statement sent to the house. Screw the parentals. Why should I tell them anything?

Of course, I picked the last days of the semester to let something set me off. It's actually good timing on my part. With exams for the semester wrapping up, me salvaging my grades, and prepping for next year's SATs, getting into trouble wouldn't hurt too much. It felt good, too, to take it out on someone who had been bothering me for a while.

Hayden Smith was one of those guys who gathered a mob of people around him. Tall, blond, popular, athletic, he was perfectly mainstream, surrounded by stylish girls and the guy friends who handled his overflow. He had a problem with, well, anyone who bothered him. And what bothered him depended on the day, the weather, and lots of other stuff I didn't even know or understand.

Hayden and I had actually been friends, believe it or not. Same crew, same parties, same friends. Except when the bills started rolling in for my brother after his last op, and I only really had time for Sara and working rather than loading up on booze with Hayden and the gang. Hayden took it as a personal insult and he hasn't let up since. I guess you could say my existence bothered him.

"Andy!" he yelled to me when I was about to make it down the hall past him.

I just ignored it. Normally, it would feel like someone was squeezing my heart in my chest. Guess the beta blockers are working. I simply walked on by, back into the crowd to be off on my way.

"Simmons!"

He ran in front of me with a slide. His friends followed, hovering at the sides in the hallway. People floated by, avoiding eye contact with me, just wanting to get past the scene that was about to happen.

"What do you want, Hayden?" I asked.

"Just wanted to know if everything's working out. You never keep in touch any more." He faked a smile. I caught a hot blonde in the back of the crowd who didn't look like she wanted to be there: Caroline. We'd only gone out for a few weeks, and she was fun as fun could be, but we both thought it wasn't a good idea to stay together, since Hayden would make her life hell for doing anything with me. This was just before Sara showed up and spun my life around. Caroline looked concerned, and I wondered if she was going to speak up, if she still liked me.

"Been busy," I said as I tried to step past. Hayden stepped back in front of me, his crew adjusting to block my way.

"Too busy for your friends?" he said. "Or got too many important things to do?"

Here he goes again. This is getting old.

"Well, yes. Too many important things to do," I said with a smile. "So, I don't want to waste time doing unimportant things, like being seen in the same town with you and your ugly girlfriend."

Hayden seethed; he liked being the center of things, the important part of everything.

A few people passing by stopped, catching what I'd said and laughing at Hayden. Caroline smiled; I smiled back.

Hayden wasn't smiling, not when people laughed at him. He stepped up, but then stopped.

"I'd give you a good beating, but you might have a brain problem like your brother..."

"Hayden," Caroline pleaded, "Just leave it alone..."

"Was it hard to pull the plug, Andy? Or did your parents rush to it because they didn't want a cripple or a stump at home? Where do you take a vegetable on vacation, by the way?"

I just kept on punching, and punching, and punching. I knew what I was doing, but I don't know why I was doing it. I didn't love my brother. He was a jerk. But then Hayden was a jerk too, and he had no idea of the kind of raw deal life had dealt my brother. Maybe there was a small part of me that wanted my brother and me to be family, real family, and it just rose to the surface.

Hayden had wanted to get a rise out of me so that he could show off to his crew; he'd got one, and a black eye and bruised cheek for it. My back was killing me from getting thrown into the wall. My arms hurt from when Hayden's friends broke us up and dragged Hayden away, getting him out of sight before any teachers arrived on the scene.

And Caroline had pulled me away from the fight, putting herself between me and Hayden, pulling at his arm when he took a swing at me. I'd forgotten how wonderful she smelled and how soft she felt.

Then she broke away from me, half-dragged by some of Hayden's boys, who scattered before a teacher showed up. She left her hand on mine for a moment longer than she should have. Her glance lingered, longer than perhaps it needed to. Even as I scrambled down the hall, I could hear Hayden yelling at Caroline for helping me.

But I could tell that she still liked me. I was sure of it.

"So, how does that make you feel?"

Do these doctors say the same damn thing all the time? This one was different, though. He didn't bitch at me about my relationship with Sara, open and strange and odd as it was.

"Good," I said. School's done for the semester, so I have a little break, even with work. I did well in classes, didn't get caught in that fight, and the job is going all right."

"And physically?"

"Better, Rich. My back still hurts from Hayden shoving me into the wall. Only been a week since the fight, but I figure another day and I'll be okay."

Dr. Richard Wright smiled, pushing up his wire-rimmed glasses. He was younger than the others, mid-thirties. He didn't give me disapproving looks. Mostly his reaction to what I told him seemed like genuine concern, and trying to find out why something had happened, and what we could do to make it better.

Maybe the other doctors were concerned as well, but I couldn't see it in them. Perhaps you just need to find the right fit between patient and doctor.

"You think it was a good reaction to Hayden?"

"Not really," I said, "thinking back on it. But it's the past."

"Yes, it is," Dr. Wright said. "Can't change it..."

"But we can learn from it," I finished his sentence.

Dr. Wright smiled. "So what did you learn?"

"Hayden doesn't like it when he doesn't seem important."

"Anything else?" Dr. Wright continued.

"I wish I could have had a normal relationship with my brother. Not necessarily love, just..." I struggled with how to word this, "a better deal on both sides. Him not hating me, me not hating him, my parents just treating us both the same."

"That's good. And it's something we can work on. So tell me more about the girl who rescued you."

"Caroline? She's pretty, and easy to talk to. Forgot how great she smells," I said. I shifted in my seat, excited just thinking about her. "I think she still likes me."

"That sounds positive," Dr. Wright said. "Are you going to try to go out with her again?"

"Hell no," I said. "Hayden's still pissed off at me, and his crew just follows. Caroline likes me, I think, but I don't think she likes me enough to deal with everyone hassling her."

"Only way you will know is if you ask."

"Yeah," I agreed. "It's just that I'm not like everyone else; especially that group. I don't really fit that well with them."

"I don't think you are so different, Andrew. You maybe need to fine tune your reactions to what people say, though. You've had a rough couple of months, on top of all the years of having had a much higher bar set for you than for your brother. It's going to take some time, but these adjustments are things we can work on together."

"Yeah. I guess."

"So you have the summer, and then your final year?"

"Yeah," I said. "Want to take at least four AP classes."

"I'm sure you are up to it. You seem bright enough. Anything still bothering you though, anything that's standing out?"

I nodded. Lots of stuff was still bothering me, but I didn't quite know where to start. Best to start small.

"My parentals are making me clean out my brother's place in New York," I told him. "I have to sort out all the stuff, list it on eBay, handle the money, and hope I get paid back for the postage and fees."

"That's a lot of work," the doctor nodded.

"Doesn't leave you much time for your summer, especially if they have you working."

"I know, but what can I do?" I shrugged.

"Have you talked to them about it? Have you let them know that you need a life of your own as well?"

"Every time I try to bring up something like that, I get told that "we all have to pull together," that "we need to be strong, we have to make some sacrifices." I guess, like you said, they keep setting the bar high for me... something needs to be done in the house, I always have to do it. Even when my brother was able to do it, it was always me they called on. My brother was the lighting tech with all the electrical experience, for example, but they'd expect me to put a new electrical socket in the wall. Made no sense at all..."

"Receiving and accepting appreciation from others is important for growth, Andrew. But how old are your parents? Fifty-five? They aren't going to change much." He scribbled a few notes. "Like I said, the best thing you can do is handle how you react, and seek other sources of appreciation, other relationships. You have your friends, like Trevor and Sara. Just work on giving other people a shot, like Caroline; try to expand friendships with classmates and co-workers and other people you might only know in passing."

I nodded. This sounded all too familiar, but at least, coming from him, it didn't sound like someone was assuming they knew what was best for me. It seemed more like, "hey, you could do this, and it could be good for you."

Dr. Wright seemed happy with my response. "And then," he said, "you won't have such a hole in your life where you feel that solid relationship with your family should have been. You'll have connections to other people, and you'll fill up that hole you think is there. It won't be easy at first, but give it time. Think you can do that?"

"Yeah, I can try that."

And after all, I thought to myself, if something came of it, it would make for smoother times until I finally came to leave this place for good

CHAPTER 6

The boys

"This lady only had the dog outside the store for, like, ten minutes, like," Trevor said, slamming the pool cue into the cue ball like thunder. The rest of the balls scattered over the pool table in his basement, two stripes rolling into two holes. Trevor's friend Bobby, lanky and lean compared to Trevor's thick wrists and bandy arms and legs, walked around the table, trying to spot any shots he would have in solids, through the bottom of his beer glass.

"She comes out of the store," Trevor lined up the three ball to a side pocket, "and she finds someone has drawn all over the thing. This little short-haired corgi with the silly short legs, all written over with, like, "slut," "Bill's Rules," and anarchy symbols. Woman dead-out faints and a priest ends up having to wake her up, like."

I watched the three ball rattle into the side pocket from the table I'm sitting at, drinking my own beer.

Trevor has a nice setup here; his dad won some money in a workers' comp lawsuit so they'd moved here from Kokomo a few years ago. His dad spent a lot of his time on vacation, picking up women half his age, so Trevor ended up having the run of the house rent-free. Trevor worked as a mechanic and did odd jobs on the side when he wasn't getting hassled by the police for "disorderly conduct."

"I mean, *I* might be disorderly according to the *law*, like," Trevor pondered as he looked at me, "but this dog's never done nothing to nobody except wait for that lady to come out of that shop."

I nodded, sketching on my computer tablet. Even with Trevor distracting me with his uniquely Hoosier wisdom, I still get more work done there than at home. And I'd shut my phone off a half-hour earlier, after the fifth call from home.

"But no, like," Trevor spat out, "those Red Bull-crazed, bitch-slapping thugs…"

"Stupid deviants," Bobby added.

"Right!" Trevor yelled, cracking his pool cue down on the edge of his pool table. "Those stupid deviants have to mess with a damn dog that didn't do a thing to them."

Trevor finished his beer, the second one in the twenty minutes we'd been there. Say what the law might about Trevor, he really didn't mess with anyone who didn't deserve all they got.

"Wish we could just go to the club," Bobby muttered.

"Well, we can't go to the club, Bobby," Trevor hissed. "Besides the fact that Andrew can't get any work done at the club, my lawyer said that if I violate my latest parole they are going to put my face on the back of a bus and might even lock me up..."

"So what's the parole for this time?" I asked.

"Cracked a few too many glasses with a pool cue," Trevor sank his shoulders. "If I'm caught underage drinking again, they're threatening to send me to juvie."

"Don't forget," Bobby chimed in as he pulled a beer from the keg tap in the basement bar, "you're not allowed to transport a woman in the front seat of your car, either."

"Well, like, thank you *Judge* Bobby," Trevor said, jabbing Bobby with the pool cue before lining up his next shot. He was off this time, the five ball bouncing around the corner.

"Not my fault I'm popular," Trevor stepped away from the table and poured another beer. "If a lady friend of mine doesn't want to wait to get where we are going..."

I waved away the beer Trevor offered me. "I can't help that. I might not be all pretty like Andrew here, but some girls consider me to be pretty exciting."

I tried not to laugh too hard; one of Trevor's first arrests was for having sex in his car while he was still driving. He made the local paper, along with an ugly barmaid. I think it's only the fact his dad has some money and because Trevor's such a likeable bastard that he's not in jail.

I met Trevor through his younger brother, Devon, in school; I don't really spend time with Devon now though, but we get along well enough. It's just more fun to be around Trevor; he doesn't care who or what you are.

"Trev," Bobby shook his head, "that girl was lucky she didn't need a dog licence."

"Hey man, Sally is a nice girl with a sweet voice," Trevor said, tackling Bobby into the wall. They tumbled around, slapping each other in the face, laughing all the way. Happy they weren't going to end up on top of my computer, I just watched the show while I put the finishing touches to a contest piece.

"Trev!" I yelled to Trevor, who had pulled his pants down and was pushing his butt into Bobby's face.

"What?" he yelled back. Bobby pushed Trevor off and scrambled away, wiping his face even though there wasn't anything on it.

"I need you to sign my dad's name on this entry form."

Trevor yanked his jeans up and walked over to me.

"I can't believe your dad won't sign these permission slips," Trevor said, taking the pen I offered him.

"What are you doing?" Bobby said, beer back in hand.

"Well, Andrew here enters these design contests," Trevor said as he looked over the permission slip in his hand. "Art stuff, graphics, like. There's money involved, so if you aren't legal yet you need to have a parent sign off on it. But Andrew's dad is a jerk who thinks these contests and exhibits are a waste of good money and won't sign off on them."

"Waste of money?" Bobby asked.

"Yeah," Trevor said, "these things have entry fees so you don't get lowlifes with markers thinking they are great *artistes*," Trevor threw up the hand with the pen in it, "flooding the judges, so that real artists don't get noticed. Andrew's already won a few of these, even making some money."

"But why won't your dad sign the forms for you," Bobby asked, "if you're making money with it?"

"Because his dad's got a stick up his butt," Trevor said as he signed a name with a flourish. "Charles A. Simmons," he announced.

I looked the signature over. It was spot on, including that stupid scribble that passed for an *R*. I nodded at Trevor, who smiled. If Trevor had an ambition, it was to become a forger. But then again, he didn't need any more legal trouble.

"And this," I said as I put a CD in an envelope, along with the form, "goes out in the mail tomorrow."

"You can buy the next keg," Trevor said. "I figure if I keep on helping you out Andrew, you'll eventually hit it big, and then I can be part of your entourage like in those rap videos."

"I hate that crap," Bobby chimed in. "Just people talking. Anyone can do it."

"Hell no," Trevor said, "They get *paid* to talk. Besides, I figure Andrew would have people playing violins 24/7 by the pool." He looked at me, a deliberate pause. "Hey Andrew, come with me; I need to get another keg out of the shed."

Trevor slapped me on the shoulder, pulled me out of my chair and pushed me along. Bobby took a step to follow, but Trevor waved him off.

The yard was pretty clean, only a few kids' toys for the various nephews who visit, cluttering up the place. A shed and a row of trash cans sat in the back. Trevor opened the lock and rolled a keg over on a handcart.

"I'm sorry," Trevor said.

"Sorry about what?" I said, wheeling the keg along. "What the fuck are you talking about, Trev?"

"I'm sorry I didn't show up at your brother's funeral."

Trevor's eyes were downcast. Like I've mentioned before, Trevor didn't show up at the funeral because he didn't know my brother.

"It's okay." I backed up the back step with the handcart and slid it out to get another keg when Trevor motioned for a second one.

"It's not okay." Trevor raised his voice. "Friends don't make excuses like that! I didn't show when you needed me."

Okay, this is new. Trevor's never been one to open up about—well, anything. He's a friend, all right, but don't expect hugs or crying, even if the Jets lose to Dallas.

"What the hell is wrong with you?"

"I should have been there," Trevor said. "Even if your parentals would have flipped out, and even if I didn't know your brother. That funeral wasn't about him. At least it wouldn't have been for me. It would have been about you, my friend, and making sure my friend was okay."

Trevor hugged me tight, patting me on the back.

"Um," is all I managed to say.

Sometimes, when you think you know your friends, you find out something you never expected. Sometimes, it's bad: your best friend is dissing you behind your back or trying to steal your girl. Sometimes, it's good, like your friend is showing you how great he is and coming through when your life is swirling down the drain. And sometimes, your friend pulls a Trevor, just reminding you what he did wrong.

Friends, parents, girls—even the police sometimes—usually let Trevor coast. I wasn't going to let him, now that he'd brought the subject up. It made me remember how pissed off I'd been that he hadn't been there for me.

"You're right, you were a dick." I shoved him away. He shoved me back.

"Yeah, maybe," Trevor said. "Don't mean you gotta remind me."

He shoved me again.

"You brought it up. No one turned up, you know! I figured *you* would have showed up just to piss off my dad!"

"He'd have just taken it out on you." Trevor knocked me into the side of the shed with a shove against my head. "Figured you didn't need that, like."

Looking back, this was all pretty silly. My friend apologizes for screwing up and I start a fight with him? Not smart, especially since Trevor had a strict training regime of bar brawls and thug-bashing. If they gave diplomas out for thuggery and hoodluming, he'd have the grades to get into Harvard. Meanwhile, I'm a damn art student with a track record of lucky punches and hurting my hand.

"You still should have shown up," I spat out.

I wrapped my hand around something nearby and swung it at Trevor. It broke over his head, glass flying everywhere. Trevor stumbled backwards, blood running from where I'd caught him. He fell over flat on his back, grasping his head.

I looked at my hand. I had grabbed a fluorescent bulb out of the trash next to the shed.

Trevor laughed, a chuckle at first but then howls of laughter.

"I deserved that one, man," Trevor said from the ground, still smiling, still bleeding. He pulled a bit of glass out of his scalp—not for the first time in his life.

I stepped toward him. Trevor held his hand up to wave me away.

"I think that makes us even," he said, "right?" He kept his hand up, ready to cover his head.

I still had the broken bulb in my hand. I tossed it back into the trash can. Trevor relaxed, rising up from the ground. He started laughing again.

"I normally get bashed with a beer mug, not a lightbulb." Trevor wiped the blood from his forehead. "We even?"

"Yeah," I said, "we're even."

And that's a friend. He might do you wrong, and it might not come up for months and months, but when it does it gets resolved and it's all water under the bridge. Even when your friend is a Hoosier, a simple guy who likes to fight too much, drink too much, and bust heads too much.

A friend is someone to connect with, right? Now that's something I haven't been able to do for a while—connect with people.

"You got a scuff on you," Trevor said, thumbing a spot on the right of my forehead.

I yelped, grabbing at what was probably the start of a bruise. I slapped his hand away.

"Now you ain't so pretty," Trevor laughed. "And I'll have a chance tonight."

"What the hell's going on out there?" Bobby cursed, coming to the back door. "Andrew, what happened to your head?"

"Just a fight," I shrugged. "What are you talking about," I said to Trevor, "a chance tonight?"

Trevor laughed again. "I mean, I'm throwing a party tonight, with lots of girls, and you all scuffed up means I've got a shot." Trevor started to roll the kegs under the bar. "I mean if you start sketching girls, they get all dreamy over you. Even if you look prettier than they do."

"Not right now he doesn't," Bobby pointed to the mirror above the bar.

Wow, I looked like hell. The bruise was only an inch or so, but my eyeliner dragged from my right eye to halfway down my cheek. I walked over to the sink at the bar and started to clean up.

"You know," Bobby said, "If I hadn't seen you making out with that girl Sara, I'd think you were gay..."

Trevor slapped Bobby in the back of the skull and shoved him forward.

"Eh, Andrew here ain't no fairy," Trevor announced as Bobby and he half-heartedly traded slaps and shoves. "Girls like them stylish or pretty, and it goes with that artist thing."

I smiled. Nice getting accepted for once. At least Trev didn't see my look as being "fag makeup."

"Wasn't saying he's a fag," Bobby said as he threw plastic soda bottles at Trevor. "Just saying they might *think* he doesn't like girls."

"Bullshit." Trevor fell over from the bottle hit, playing dead on the floor. "Don't matter what they think. Live your life. My dad's off on some island with a girl half his age. "Scandalous," everyone says. They can all go to hell. Just live your life, don't hurt people that don't deserve a beating, and watch out for your friends. Don't worry about what the rest of the world thinks, they aren't living your life for you."

I stopped in mid-touchup. Trevor was right. Why the hell was I worrying about what the parentals think? Or Hayden or his snobby friends? Just do the stuff I do, and the people who want to stick around will stick around.

"Genius, Trevor, genius..."

"Damn right I am," Trevor said. "It's why I hang around with you—I get smarter every day!"

Trevor hopped over the sofa and fumbled for the TV remote.

"Bobby, get the food together. Football's on soon, and we got some people heading over."

And I realize that people would want to be around me if I just let them. And all I had to do was be myself and not worry so much.

CHAPTER 7

Go with the flow

The great thing about Emma is that she's very soft and cuddly. This I know because she was half on my lap on the sofa. Not like anything much was going to happen, but I wasn't going to throw an attractive girl, pressing up against me, out the door. She also loved football and didn't give a damn what anyone thought, so she fitted in well with Trevor, Bobby, and the rest of Trevor's hoodlums and pals.

Trevor ignored the plastic bottle—thrown by Emma—banging into his head. He was too busy watching Brunell throw a perfect pass to notice Emma's glare.

"Trev, how could you maim the boy like this?" Emma brushed away a loose strand and hovered her fingers over the bruise, before she went back to stroking my hair.

"Just a friend's fight," Trevor said, not even looking back. "He's still prettier than me."

"Yes," Emma said, "yes he is." And she continued her gentle stroking.

I could get used to this. And I keep on hearing Sara screaming in my head *just jump her NOW!!!* and I can barely stop laughing. Emma took this to be solely her work, which I had no problem with right then. I leaned in a bit and watched the Jets intercept a pass, keeping it out of Dallas's reach.

Melanie, Neil's girl, handed the plastic bottle back to Emma. Emma hurled it, cap-end-first, once again catching Trevor square in the head. Trevor finally spun around.

"Look, it's over and everyone is okay with…"

Trevor suddenly snapped back to the TV. "Go go go go go go—YES!!!" he roared as the running back rocketed past the opposition. Everyone joined him in cheering the Jets' second touchdown of the game.

Neil, a lanky salesman for an electronics store, immediately sent a text to taunt his brother, a die-hard Dallas fan. Bobby and his younger brother George punched each other while singing Queen's "We Will Rock You" off key and with additional lyrics.

And as always, I just took it all in. This time though, I was in the middle of it, rather than sitting outside. Part of the action instead of just watching it and wondering why I wasn't included. I thought back, through the better filter I now had since talking to my doctor, and realized that part of it wasn't just people ignoring me or hating me. Some of it was how I reacted, or overreacted a lot of the time. People didn't want to deal with the drama, with the way I'd get angry when things didn't pan out right.

I mean, it wasn't *all* my fault. But some of it was, and that was mostly down to the way I reacted to things. Looking back, even to stuff when I was young, I could see where I went wrong on some things. Some of it was damn stupid, too.

My phone rang. Trevor had it—he'd said he needed to call someone earlier, but it couldn't be from his phone. Trevor held the phone out to me without looking at it, but pulled it away every time I grabbed for it. I managed to get it away from him after Emma slapped his hand.

Dad.

I had half a mind just to shut the phone off, or scream at him, but I remembered what I'd just been thinking about.

"Excuse me," I said as I slid Emma off me and found a quiet hallway near the stairs. "Hello," I said calmly.

"Andrew, where in God's name are you?"

It was my dad all right, his voice going from Zero to Yelling in two point two seconds. I held the phone away, taking a moment to think of what to say next.

"I'm okay, Dad. I'm out with friends."

"You really need to come home now." He lowered his yelling voice to "very concerned," the one all parents use to trick their kids.

Or maybe he *was* concerned. Don't assume he's out to get you, I thought. I paused again before I spoke.

"That's not going to happen. I'm safe somewhere, and I'll be home sometime soon. Tomorrow, during the day."

"Don't you use that tone with me!"

I thought about it, pretty sure I didn't use any "tone." He was angry, and had a pretty good reason to be too, since I'd clocked him. I needed to head this off.

"Dad, put Mom on."

"Your mom is very upset and in no condition to talk to you! You need to get home…"

"Dad, either give the phone to Mom or I will be ending this call."

Silence.

I continued, taking a breath first.

"I'm willing to discuss all this another time," I said, being careful with the words, "but right now I need to be here, where I am. I'm safe at a friend's place, and I'm going to be staying overnight. Now put Mom on and I will try to calm her down."

Silence, then sobbing.

"Mom?"

"Andrew," a voice broke over the phone.

"Mom," I said, "just letting you know I'm somewhere safe, okay?"

More crying. Just as bad as at William's funeral, actually.

"Mom," I said, "just breathe in deep a few times, and then we'll talk, okay?"

The crying continued, followed by a few wheezing breaths. When I was sure she was listening again, I started speaking.

"Mom, like I said, I'm safe. I'm with some friends and I'm going to be here the night, okay."

Some sniffling over the phone again.

"I need this time away," I said. "It's been rough for everyone. There's stuff we're all going to have to talk about. But right now isn't a good time for that. So I'm going to come back tomorrow and we're going to sit down and talk about things, okay?"

"Okay," Mom managed to push out.

"Just tell Dad I'm safe, inside, and that the Jets just got a second touchdown."

Mom laughed. Dad probably already knew, since he was such a fan. Shit though—he'd called during the game. He never let anything interrupt a Jets game. No e-mails, no phone calls... once, he'd made a director of a technology company watch the game with him while they worked on product guidelines. When I was younger we watched football all the time. Once, we went to Boston to see the Jets play the Patriots—that was William, Dad and me. Later on, when William was in the hospital, we'd sit and talk about the team, and that was about the only time we talked. It was one of the things Dad and I used to get away from everything that hurt. We'd just turn to football and hope for the best for William. It never lasted long, spending time with Dad, but it did happen.

There was good stuff. But it takes some digging and thinking about, and things happening, to bring it all out. But there was good stuff going on in our lives. Like the Jets games, and this dinner we had in Spain where the waiters went around with a pitcher of wine and poured it right into your mouth until you couldn't drink any more.

Dad drank the whole thing and they had to bring a second one out, which he got halfway through before he had to come up for air.

"I'll let him know," Mom said, interrupting my thoughts. "He shut the game off when he called you."

"Mom?"

"Yes?"

"We'll work this out, okay?"

"I love you, Andrew," she said, and that was the end of the call.

I've never been one to say "I love you" or things like that. I think the only person I ever *said* it to was Sara, and even that caught her off guard. I always want to hear it, and I certainly feel it. However I just don't usually say it though. I'd rather *do* stuff to show that I care about people. Some people just say it easily, and meanwhile they're running around on their boyfriends and girlfriends, talking about them behind their backs, or trying to mess up their lives. That's not love or caring about someone. That's playing a game.

The phone rang again.

"Mom, I said I'd be home tomorrow..."

"Do I sound like your mother?" Sara said with a laugh.

This is what I get for not looking at the screen before answering; Sara's number was flashing on the display.

"Hey baby doll!"

"Greetings from the past!" she yelled at me. "Whatcha doing?"

"Just off the phone with the parentals. I decked my Dad earlier today."

"Oh my God, you okay? What happened?"

"Just a fight. I think it passed," I said. "We're going to talk it out tomorrow when I get home."

"You're actually going to talk to your parents about real things?"

"Yeah," I said. "Just figure it's time to try to work this all out. I've been a pain in the ass to them."

"Maybe you have, love."

"Gee, thanks..."

"What I mean is that Will's death bothered you, too, and you never really got to talk to them about it. Or talked about his life. So it's good if you do."

"Yeah. There's stuff I can do better."

"We can all do stuff better," Sara said. "Anyway, what are you up to tonight?"

"I'm at Trevor's house. We're watching the Jets game."

"Ooh, is that girl Emma there? You should so have sex with her and take pics."

I smiled. It was great to have a personal cheerleader in my life.

"I *could* do that... but I don't think it's that kind of thing. She does like sitting in my lap though."

"Damn you, I want lap-sitting!" she pouted over the phone.

"You can sit on my lap when you visit next..."

"No, I meant her in my lap!"

Well, at least Sara knows what she wants... which is everything.

"Gee, thanks..."

"Oh, I fully intend to share her. You can have her every other weekend."

"And you get her all the rest of the time?" I asked.

"We'll send her away so that we have

time together," she reassured me.

"I love you, you know that?" Easy for me to say to her, not so easy for me to say to anyone else.

"Yep," she said cheerily. "So, just your football game today?"

"Yes, football," I said. "And a party tonight."

"You mean you are actually going out and interacting with people? They grow up so fast..." She sniffed fake tears over the phone. I laughed at her.

"You know that I actually *do* go out and do stuff, right?"

"Yes, I know. But it's my job to tease you about everything while hoping you take naked pictures of the girls you seduce."

"I'll do what I can tonight, okay?"

"You'd better," she warned, "or I'm just

going to have to find myself another pretty gothed-up artist to play with."

"I love you too."

And this is why Sara rocks so much. A sexy drugged angel asleep in bed with a soul as strong as steel. A voice of reason when I need one, a cheerleader and biggest fan the rest of the time. That's love and understanding.

And I realized she wasn't the only one who felt that way about me. Trevor, and Emma... and my parentals. I might not have always understood the ways they tried to care, and they might not have been good at expressing it. But if Dad was willing to shut off the New York Jets to talk to me after I'd punched him, maybe it was a start.

Still, at that time all I wanted was to finish watching Jets beat Dallas, with a cute girl in my lap.

Trev's house is pretty big, but it's still amazing how many people he can manage to get in it. He crammed about fifty people in there, not including the people in the yard. It was a good mix of people my age— college students, mechanics from where Trev worked, and a few older people that fitted in well with the group. Like I said before, everyone ended up liking Trevor whether they wanted to or not.

I wasn't much for crowds, so the party was stressing me out a bit. I tried to hang around the people I knew best, like Trevor, Emma, and a few others. People were friendly enough; it's just that when the mobs of people started to wade on in, I got a bit anxious. It's not like I thought I was going to screw up when I said stuff. Just more like not quite knowing what to say and how it was going to sound.

"You," Trevor grabbed me by the shoulders and spun me around, "need to drink a bit more." He put a beer in my hand.

"You're probably right," I laughed.

"Relax," he shook me while he talked. "Nothing you do here will end up on the front page of the *Daily News* or the police blotter. That's reserved for me."

"I'm not a crowd person."

"I know," Trevor said. "But don't think of it as crowds. There just happen to be a few groups of a few groups. Focus on what's right in front of you. Like these hoodlums all the way down from Buffalo," Trevor dragged me over to two husky, but cute girls. "They go to SUNY and play hockey, friends of my cousins." He introduced me to them. "Teresa, Melanie, this is Andrew. He's an artist, so don't hurt his hands or anything."

"Did you punch him?" Teresa shot Trevor a look while she reached out to the bruise on my head. I resisted the urge to pull away from a surprisingly light touch.

"Yeah, yeah, I know... "Trevor, you punched him? You're a damn wimp, screw you, piss off, you bad bad man..."' Trevor exaggerated his ranting to defuse anything the girls might be planning to say.

"It's okay, the boy's tougher than he looks. Andrew, you should tell them how you punched your dad today. Have to run and finish setting something up."

And there I was, dropped in the middle of things, just talking about stuff. And people listened, with a small crowd just getting in on things. Other people jumped in, from one of Trevor's friends at work, talking about how he and his brother went through a plate glass window in a fight, to Teresa showing off the scar she got in a pretty nasty hockey game.

People listened to what I said, and they teased me too. But I didn't get mad at the goth makeup cracks or the getting a "real man's job" jokes. I either let it slide or threw it back at them that they were just upset because I was prettier than their girlfriends. Everyone laughed, everyone drank, everyone had fun. I just mingled, talking to and listening to everyone, taking a little time to tease Emma a bit, and watch Trevor move an impromptu wrestling match out to the yard...

And I fit right in.

Part of that was just relaxing, and part of it was not caring what people thought. I wouldn't see most of these people ever again, so what did anything matter? Besides, despite years of thinking otherwise, most people weren't actively trying to mess with my day. They couldn't know the stuff I was going through in my life, just like I didn't know the stuff going on in theirs.

And as for the Hayden Smiths of the world who wanted to get a rise out of me, or the people just trying to cause trouble? Well, you'll always run into those people, and you can either flip out over it or do your best to not let it bother you. Chances are you won't be around those people for the rest of your life. For one thing, once school wraps up, Hayden's going to be a distant memory. I mean, there will always be people like him, but there are far more people like Trevor and Emma and Sara in the world. If I come across a Hayden, I'll just cross the street.

And people kept handing me beers. I was pretty good about holding my liquor and I kept an eye on what I drank, but it's one of the downsides of just fitting in, I discovered, that people keep handing you drinks. I took my time with them, and ate stuff to slow down the alcohol, but I could feel the buzz running through me. I avoided the urge to drunk-text Sara, even though I wanted her to know I was having a good time; she could call and I'd tell her all about it during the week.

"You!" Trevor grabbed me and pulled me away from his boss, who was looking to make a new logo for the auto shop and picking my brains.

"What?" I slurred, as Trevor pushed me up the stairs.

"Got a surprise for you," Trevor laughed.

"I'm not big on surprises," I said.

"You'll like this one," Trevor assured me. "I arranged it special. Consider it me making up for the bruise."

We kept on going upstairs, to the top floor that Trevor had blocked off with a few chairs. He'd scrawled a note—OFF LIMITS OR I'LL HURT YOU—it said, and taped it to a chair. We stopped at his dad's bedroom, where Trevor had put my laptop so it wouldn't get smashed by accident.

"Gotta make sure we're still good on beer," Trevor said. He turned the knob of the door and shoved me inside.

Trevor's dad's room was a shrine to the Jets, from autographed pictures going back to the seventies, to a piece of the stadium in a shadow box. Caroline stood in front of the glass box, staring at it curiously.

"Some guys are more serious about football than others," I mumbled.

Caroline jumped, not having realized I was there. I tried not to laugh, but she giggled first.

"I got a call from Trevor out of the blue today," she said. "I don't know how he got my number. Told me to show up without "that tool Hayden and his fools" because you wanted to talk to me."

I'm going to kill Trevor, I thought. Or thank him. I don't know which yet.

"He got it off my phone today, I guess."

"You still have my number on your phone, Andrew?"

"Yeah." I tried not to make eye contact. "Just never took it off."

"Oh, okay," Caroline said, her voice dropping.

Think quick...

"And I thought I might, you know, want to call you again. See how you were doing."

"I'm good. Just another year of school and then college."

"Yeah. The AP classes and exams and then figuring out where to go..."

And then it was quiet. She didn't say anything; I didn't say anything. And in the back of my mind, Trevor and Sara were both screaming at me to do *something*.

"We should have kept on seeing each other," I said. She nodded in agreement, even before I'd finished talking.

"Why didn't we?" she said.

I thought about this for a moment. We had been so worried about what other people thought, and I had been going nuts dealing with my family, and I was just an idiot, and...

"I don't know," I said. "Don't care though. It's the past."

"Yeah," she said, smiling. "You still... I mean, you want to go out? I mean, sometime?"

"Yeah."

She sat on the bed. So did I. We talked. Beer was really getting to me, but I remember some of the stuff that happened—the good, and the bad. Mostly, it was just getting to know each other, talking and seeing that we had stuff in common, like art and music. She was with Hayden's crowd because everyone was nice to her, but it bothered her that they weren't nice to me. Hayden also liked her, even though he had a girlfriend, and that was causing all sorts of problems. I told her I didn't give a damn what Hayden thought any more. And she was a great kisser, just like I remembered.

That was the good.

The bad was Hayden finding out about

the party and finding out that I was upstairs. The bad was also Hayden finding the two of us wearing just enough clothing to spare the modesty of one person.

Like I said, I don't remember much. I woke up the next morning next to Caroline. She assured me it hadn't been anything other than us in the same bed sleeping. I was glad about that, because I wasn't in a rush, and neither was she. My head hurt like hell, so the next hour was Caroline rubbing my temples and talking with me about lots of different things. We wandered downstairs to find most of the house trashed beyond recognition. This was a sign of a good party at Trevor's, for whom success was based on how many people were passed out, and how many days it took him to clean up. At least Trevor had the sense to drag most of the drunks unable to get home into the house from the yard, neatly lining them up in the basement downstairs.

"So yeah, Hayden heard about the party," Trevor said between forkfuls of eggs, "and someone must have told him they saw you here, heading upstairs." He nodded at Caroline. "He brought a few of his friends with him and didn't take it well finding you two in bed together. When I got upstairs, he had already got some good shots in on you."

That explained why my stomach hurt so much. I looked under my shirt, seeing the ugly purple bruise along my ribs. Caroline gasped while Trevor shrugged it off.

"But you got the better of him, Andrew."

"I did?"

"Yeah," Trevor laughed. "Kicked right in the nuts..."

Trevor then mimed the fight, including the part where I punted Hayden down the stairs while I was yelling "I don't give a damn what you think!" over and over again. I kept my head low, trying not to be too embarrassed when Trevor described how I vomited all over Hayden just as he tried to hit me with a lamp. Caroline smiled, remembering it and everything else all too well.

"Anyway," Trevor continued after a last kick into the imaginary Hayden on the floor, "my cousins' friends and a few others took him out back and, like, worked him over after they ripped his pants off. Then we handed him back to his friends, and said if they called the cops we'd set their cars on fire. Don't think he's going to live down two hockey girls beating the creap out of him."

Trevor paused for a moment. "You two look really cute together."

I laughed, even through the pain of my ribs and the hangover. Caroline smiled and took hold of my hand under the table. I could get used to this. Especially the "hey, I'm dating someone" part. I can, of course, do without the "oh God, my ribs are on fire" part...

Trevor loaded us up with food and juice, which I for one really needed. I still had to talk to my parents later. It wasn't going to be easy, and the yelling that would probably happen wasn't going to be good for my head.

But at least the parentals were going to listen this time. Wish they'd listened sooner. But that was in the past. They *were* going to listen to me this time.

CHAPTER 8

Family, friend, friend of family

Blog Entry For: Andrew Simmons
Mood: Pissed Off
July 15, 6:22 p.m. Private

I wasn't sure how this was going to turn out or what I'd want to write here. No one else gets to read it, not even Sara, so I can say whatever I want. Learned a lot in the past few days, or maybe I just realized stuff I learned months or years ago. Not going to try to be too deep here, but maybe I'll look back at it years from now and it will seem deep for a sixteen-year-old.

The party was great, even with the surprises. I'm not one for surprises, or ambushes or anything like that, but Trevor outdid himself.

Caroline and I talked about lots of things, and I'm remembering the bits and pieces about pounding Hayden now that I'm sober. I'm remembering kissing Caroline and a lot more, and I'm remembering just lying in bed with her and talking. I don't know if we're "dating" yet, but we're going to talk some more tomorrow and see what's what.

I showered at Trevor's and got cleaned up. When I could pass for sober, he dropped me off about two streets from my house and wished me luck. Then, the walk to my door, about 11 am.

Dad hugged me when I came in, but then he pulled away when he remembered I didn't like people touching me. I said it was okay and dropped my bag in the living room. He asked me about the bruise on my head. I just told him it was a fight between friends, nothing special. Mom came in and hugged me. I did everything I could not to yell from the pain in my ribs.

We talked. It was a lot of talking—at least from me. Mostly it was me telling them to let me say what I needed to say. Dad kept on wanting to interrupt, but I told him he just had to listen. I know William didn't like me, based on what he said and did. I didn't hate him, but I didn't really love *him* either. I knew he'd got a suck deal from life, and he took lots of it out on me. I knew that he needed a lot more attention and stuff than I did, needed a lot more help. And I knew that they understood him a lot better than they understood me. I'd had to come second.

But it still didn't mean that I didn't want stuff, or attention, or love. Just because I was able to do stuff on my own didn't mean I didn't want them to pay attention to what I did. And part of that was down to me too, I know. I just didn't click with them. I'm not the sort of person to say that I care about people, and I think that makes me seem cold; I make sure the trash cans are out and I clean up after myself. I'd left everyone alone when William got sick and had his operations. And I shouldn't have done that. I should have spoken up more, should have pushed more, because that would have been better for everyone. I shouldn't have let William take stuff out on me, I should have been louder and angrier and I should have stood up for myself.

I could have handled things better too, I know that. And I made sure that Dad and Mom knew that. But I wanted them to know that I am still here, and that for all their talk about "pitching in" and "helping out," they sometimes forget that. I need to know they want me here. It took a while, but I got all this across to them.

This is when Dad started crying. He was angry and red, and his hands shook. Mom wanted to get up and leave, but I told her we needed to do this now or it wasn't ever going to get resolved. I said it again, because they needed to hear it: William never really showed me that he cared, despite what they said or thought. William was angry with me for some reason, but I couldn't help being me, just like he couldn't help being him.

I just wanted to hear that I was doing the right things—someone telling me, "hey, you aren't screwing up." Sometimes they'd done that, but I'd had nowhere near the kind of support from them that William had. Just because William had had a tougher mountain to climb didn't mean that I had had an easy walk of it.

So I just put it all out there and said we should see about all of us finding someone to talk to about this. We could go to support groups for parents who had lost kids, we could talk with friends. We could even just talk about it together from time to time. I'd buried stuff for too long, they'd kept on trying to keep everything and everyone together on the surface, without seeing what it was that was actually pulling us apart...

It kind of dropped off from there and these are just the headlines—the whole conversation went on a bit. But I think that some of it got through. We got Italian takeout that night, and we actually sat at a table and ate together. Mom talked about some real estate deals, Dad talked about projects at work. They asked me how work was for me, and if I had painted anything recently. We didn't talk about William.

We talked about us.

Family, friend, friend of family

GraphicAndrew: *wave*

HaveYouSeenMyPants: Hey love

HaveYouSeenMyPants: How was the party?

GraphicAndrew: It was good...

HaveYouSeenMyPants: *plays porno music*

HaveYouSeenMyPants: hehehehe

GraphicAndrew: stop that. :P

HaveYouSeenMyPants: well, I figured you would have hooked up with Emma at least...

GraphicAndrew: nononono...

HaveYouSeenMyPants: :(

GraphicAndrew: Caroline was there

HaveYouSeenMyPants: you mean the blonde girl? The stylish one?

GraphicAndrew: yeah

HaveYouSeenMyPants: *turns up porno music*

HaveYouSeenMyPants: ;)

GraphicAndrew: No no no...

GraphicAndrew: sort of...

HaveYouSeenMyPants: oooooooo...

HaveYouSeenMyPants: do tell...

GraphicAndrew: we were in bed. Talking mostly. Some other stuff

HaveYouSeenMyPants: did you get pictures?

GraphicAndrew: no. :P

HaveYouSeenMyPants: damn :)

GraphicAndrew: it's a good start

HaveYouSeenMyPants: so you gonna see her again?

GraphicAndrew: yeah. Gonna see what happens with us. At least give it a shot

HaveYouSeenMyPants: hey, isn't she one of Hayden's friends?

GraphicAndrew: was, I think. I think I convinced her not to care after I beat Hayden up at Trevor's party

HaveYouSeenMyPants: !!!!!!!!!!!!!!!!!!!!!

GraphicAndrew: don't remember much, I was drunk. Trevor said I pounded Hayden and threw him down some stairs

HaveYouSeenMyPants: rock!

GraphicAndrew: gonna email you something, just read it and delete it, OK?

HaveYouSeenMyPants: OK

GraphicAndrew: sent

The Only Brother

HaveYouSeenMyPants: *waits*

HaveYouSeenMyPants: got it, gimme a sec

HaveYouSeenMyPants: OMG *hugs*

GraphicAndrew: I do the right thing?

HaveYouSeenMyPants: I think you did

GraphicAndrew: I'm surprised I didn't get thrown out of the house

HaveYouSeenMyPants: I don't think they want to lose another son

GraphicAndrew: I don't think they want to lose me. Not just "another son." They actually talked to me about what I was doing. May seem a bit late, but the past is, well... past. Time to be part of the family

HaveYouSeenMyPants: yeah

HaveYouSeenMyPants: I love you, you know that?

GraphicAndrew: yep. Never doubted it

GraphicAndrew: love you too

GraphicAndrew: I'm gonna go and get some sleep. Last night and today were rough

HaveYouSeenMyPants: *hops into bed with you*

GraphicAndrew: hehehehe

HaveYouSeenMyPants: sleep well, dear

A few weeks before the start of the semester, I got a call from a number I didn't recognize. Turned out it was Buzz.

"Namaste, Andrew," he said.

"Hey Buzz," I said. "I'm not home right now, but if you lost my parents' number I can give it ..."

"Actually, I needed to talk to you." He cut me off as politely as possible.

"Oh, okay," I said. "What's up?"

"I'm going to be visiting in a few weeks, wrapping up the trust account, reading the will, things like that. It's something we should have done earlier, but with everything being so stressful for your parents, I didn't think it was a good idea to rush right into it. I need to meet with you beforehand, though."

"Okay..." Now I was wondering what was going on.

"It's nothing bad," Buzz assured me. "Just want to see how you are doing."

"I'm better. Working through stuff with the family. It's not easy, you know?"

"Yeah," he said, his Jersey accent loud and clear. "I know. I know I miss William. I know your parents do."

"Yeah," I agreed.

"I know you had problems with him, Andrew. And he had problems with you."

I paused.

"It's okay, Andrew. I know you guys didn't click. Sometimes that happens. But we'll talk about this more when I see you, okay? I'm going to call your parents and give them my flight info. Do me a favor?"

"Um, yeah?"

"Don't tell your parents about me wanting to meet with you ahead of time, okay?"

"Sure."

Buzz hung up, leaving me with a head full of questions. From what I know, Buzz is not much for secrets. They stay in touch, him, Dad and Mom, and for him to hide something from them it has to be something serious.

I thought about calling him again to see if he'd just tell me, but thought better of it.

Instead I headed over to Caroline's to meet her parents. She'd warned them about the makeup and pushed that I was a working artist, so figured that I should go over well. Next week is her meeting my parents. I don't have to explain anything to my parents, they are just glad that I'm bringing someone home.

It was not turning out to be a bad life, all in all.

CHAPTER 9

Showing, not telling

Buzz walked into a different Simmons family than the one he'd left back in April. We were talking to each other, for one thing. It wasn't all hugs and sunshine, but at least I wasn't locking myself in my room all the time, and Dad wasn't getting in the way of my fist. Mom had dropped back into work, like she always did, and Dad spent half the time speaking to Canadian people on the phone. But when we were depressed, or angry or confused, we talked about it. We'd found a family counselor to walk us through things.

That didn't go so well. Dad's not one to talk to people he doesn't know, so it was mostly him being quiet for an hour and then going on and on as soon as we walked out of the door. But at least he's talking about stuff that's bothering him, and not just Will's death. It's like someone's opened a floodgate to let out things he's kept bottled up all the time. The parentals fight a bit more, but at least they get it out of the way and realize that they still like each other. Dad has also found a group for parents who have lost children, and that's helped him a lot.

And at least they now understand how I feel, even if they don't agree with what I'm saying. Will never really showed that he cared much about me, and I'm fine with that. Like I've said, some people just don't get along, and being related to them doesn't make much of a difference. Will had a rough life, and lots of problems. I wish things had been better, and that he hadn't resented me so much, and I wish I could have handled the situation better.

But that's all in the past. Nothing you can do about it, so you should look forward. Which is what we did. I started to research universities, and I worked and got ready for my last year of school. I knew that I'd probably end up staying in the states with money being so tight, but I didn't feel that I needed to flee the country any more anyway. I could stand being with my parentals again, and they didn't always wonder why I wasn't part of the family.

Buzz wanted a private place to meet me, away from my parents. Trevor had let me use his house for many things, from a private place for Caroline and me, to a mailing address for my contest entries. I had a key, so I just met Buzz there. Buzz wasn't a drinker but he didn't say anything about my pouring a beer from the tap.

"So what's the big secret, Buzz?" I sprawled out on the sofa downstairs in the barroom.

Buzz looked at me, exhausted. Exhausted for him, that is. Actually, he only seemed slightly tired for someone straight off a five-hour flight and still jet-lagged. He had stacks of papers in a bag, all different kinds of documents and forms, and spread some of them out on the table.

"It's not a secret, Andrew." Buzz made some notes on a legal pad. "I just thought it best to let you know about what is going to happen, before we sit together with your parents to announce it all formally. I didn't want to catch you off guard when it all comes out."

"All right," I said, "so what's going on?"

"We read your brother's will next week. Once we execute the will and it is certified, we can get money into the trust account, pay off the last of the bills, get money back to your parents and disburse the rest of the estate."

"Okay," I said. "What does this have to do with me?"

"Come here, Andrew."

I put my beer down and sat at the table. Buzz slid a document across the table to me, neatly folded in a textured envelope.

"Last Will and Testament," I read from the envelope.

"Read it," he told me.

I took the will out of the envelope and opened it.

"'I, William Simmons,'" I read aloud, "'declare this to be my will, and I revoke any and all wills and codicils I previously made.'"

"Go on," Buzz said.

"'I direct my executors to pay my enforceable unsecured debts and funeral expenses, the expenses of my last illness, and the expenses of administering my estate. I bequeath all my tangible personal property and all policies and proceeds of insurance covering such property in the following manner: Andrew Simmons, seventy-five percent; Richard and Margaret Simmons, twenty-five percent.'"

I put the will down.

"Okay," I said. "My parentals told me just to use the laptop. We've already sold off William's car, though, to pay for the funeral and the medical bills. I mean, what else is there?"

"They never told you, did they?"

"Told me what?" I said.

"You know how your brother got his nerve damage?"

"Yeah, from the delivery, when he was born," I said. "Messed up his motor skills, made it hard for him to do things. Maybe it even caused all the other medical problems later on."

"Well, Will ended up with a settlement from the doctor and the hospital. From their insurance, actually. You probably don't remember much about it, since you were young during all of the legal wrangling. Anyway, Will set up a trust for you."

"What?"

"He wasn't good at telling people that he cared about them," Buzz said. "And he knew how you lost out all the time. All the attention, all the money spent on him, all the... well, everything. He had lots of problems, some we saw and some he kept hidden. He wasn't good at dealing with people or letting them know how he felt about them, like I said. And that hurt him."

I could understand all of that. William wasn't good with people at all. Grew up without lots of friends, got made fun of all the time because he was so clumsy, because of his weight and... well, lots of stuff. When they got to know him, people usually thought he was a pretty good person. I wish the same could be said of me.

"Well, yeah, he never really showed *me* he cared. Can't help it now. We just didn't fit together."

"He left you a trust fund, Andrew." Buzz dug through his papers, pulling out a financial statement. "He set it up out of the money he got from the settlement. Outside of university expenses and medical needs, you can't touch it until you are twenty-five. But he left you this," Buzz said as he handed me the paper.

It was a financial statement for a trust fund. From what I could tell, it was established by William when he came of legal age. Right now, it had over $400,000 in it.

I was the sole beneficiary of the trust fund. No one else can legally touch the money. Not my parentals. It was all mine.

"He never knew how to show his true feelings for you, Andrew. He felt that he could never say the words," Buzz said, "and that you would never listen to him anyway. He was just as frustrated as you were, with himself and with the world. Somehow, I figured out how to talk to him. He was my friend. He wanted to show you how much he cared, and how bad he felt about you losing out on everything just because *he* hadn't come out right. So he took what he had, a big chunk of it, and arranged things so you wouldn't lose out when it mattered."

That was Will's money. I'd heard about the settlement, but no one talked about it. I didn't know how much it had come to. And the parentals hadn't been able to touch this part of it for his medical bills, because he'd set it up for me. That's why everything had been so tight later on.

Damn.

"He knew that he was sick and that he might not live all that long. Even if he did live through everything, he didn't want the money. He had enough from his work, and anyway, it just reminded him of how messed up he felt. What he didn't have was a brother he could understand, or who understood him. So he tried to find a way to make it up to you. Make up for the money and time. Well, the money at any rate."

Damn.

"You two were different, really. Except for the caring about people part." Buzz shuffled through more papers. "That you both did, in your own way. I see William every time I look at you, Andrew."

DAMN!

Buzz let me run off to the bathroom. He didn't knock on the door to see if I was okay when I threw up in the sink. He didn't try to open the door when I sat on the floor and cried so loud you could hear me in the hall.

I know why Buzz was a good friend to my brother. Buzz knew when you needed him, and when you needed to be alone. Right then, I needed to be alone.

I came out of the bathroom after about twenty minutes. Buzz was sitting in the same spot where I'd left him, waiting to speak when I was ready to listen. I sat back down across from him, slumped.

"Your parents know about the trust, but not how much is in it. They shouldn't have a problem with the will, though. He always talked to them about how bad he felt, and how he could and would make things better for you."

Back in the bathroom, back to throwing up.

And he tied up all that money for me rather than spend it on his medical bills. Tied it all up so only I would have it, in a trust that meant no one else could take the money. Not the parentals, not anyone.

But why had the parentals gone along with it?

Because they didn't want to take money intended for me? Because that would have been them always giving to William and taking from me?

Damn...

Will *had* cared, then. He'd never said it, never showed it. Or maybe I just couldn't or wouldn't see it. He'd never told me "hey,

I'm leaving you a fortune, sorry about everything." It was like we were speaking two different languages and screaming at each other when we were together, just because we didn't make any effort to understand each other.

Damn.

What's past is past.

Now, and for all time, I know that I had—have—a brother who *did* care.

We certified the will the following week. My parents didn't freak out over the details of the will, no questioning of the amounts or the trust. I figure that they must have been involved in drafting it. Damn. They'd known all along. If only they'd told me. But I can imagine that Will had sworn them to secrecy. The trust was mine with some law firm overseeing it.

My parents and I never talked about the money after that. It was there for when I needed it. That was going to be for school expenses, and planning ahead, figuring out where to go to college. It was a lot of money for the future. Maybe a house, maybe start a business after college. See how things go with Caroline if I stay here.

And maybe find a way to show Will that *I* cared about him, too.

CHAPTER 10

A million lumen life

It was clear glass, six inches thick and translucent, three feet tall. I had to arrange special permission to use glass rather than granite, but we all fought for it. The design was mine, with a company in San Francisco carving and shipping it here. I set up a series of solar-powered LED lights to shine on the glass, a perfect display for day or night.

The logo was simple, a silhouette of a man standing in a Super-Trouper spotlight, shining down from a theater lighting truss. The man held his arms up triumphantly; the spotlight bore a cross. Over the top of the spotlight it said

"William Simmons" in elegant text. Under the logo of the man in the spotlight, it read "A Million Lumen Life," and to me, to all of us, that represents the brilliance of the light that Will's life had brought to the world. To either side read his date of birth and date of death.

I ran my hand over the words, first William's name and then the words underneath. I used my sleeve to wipe away the tiniest of smudges, polishing and brushing away errant fall leaves from a nearby tree.

"How much did it cost, Andrew?"

I turned back and looked over my shoulder at Sara, who had flown over to visit for her holiday break. She shivered a bit in the cold, brushing dark hair from her face and bundling up again. She stared at my work, finally seeing face to face the design that had struck me in the middle of the night and had kept me up until sunrise working on it.

"Just the right amount for what it is," I said, avoiding mention of the actual price. "Forget the cost."

I stepped back and looked over the lone pillar of glass in a sea of granite and marble. It stood out, just like William. Different, strange, not quite fitting in with the rest. But still having its place, still reminding people that it was there and special and important.

Just like William.

"It's beautiful."

"It got me into Pratt Institute," I said. "The admissions board said it was "a unique tribute that showed remarkable potential." Guess it's another gift from William."

"How did your parents handle it? I mean, the tombstone?"

"They both cried," I said slowly. "We all did. Dad loved the lights, said William would have taken them apart and put them back together. They probably wouldn't have worked afterward, but Will would have just wired up a new set of lights ten times as bright." I smiled, making a shadow puppet on the glass for a brief moment.

I remembered Will making shadow puppets pretending to eat my head when I was younger; big shadows on the wall biting my shadow-head. I'd forgotten about it a long time ago, but it popped back into my mind as the big shadow dog I'd made chomped on the little man in the spotlight. It's good to remember these things now, stuff I'd blocked out when I focused on all the bad things.

"What about school?"

"They said I had to do what was right for me. Mom cried, again, but Dad was pleased I'd found something that could make me money and make me happy."

Sara put her hand on my shoulder. I put my hand over hers.

"They thought the same thing about Will doing lighting design. "How are you going to make a living lighting up people on stage wearing too much makeup?'" I said in my best imitation of my dad's voice. "He showed Dad to be wrong, so I at least get a chance to show that I can make my own way now."

"Yeah," Sara said, kneeling down behind me and wrapping her arms around me. We just looked at the tombstone for a few minutes before she spoke again.

"Lots of people are going to miss you here, Andrew."

"Yeah," I said. "Trevor wants to visit, said he wants to go to Las Vegas too."

"Las Vegas is thousands of miles away from Brooklyn..."

"I know that," I laughed. "But he's seen the commercials and thinks they don't have cops there for some reason."

"Glad you have enough money to bail him out," she said. "And Caroline?"

"Well, not everything works out. She's going to Berkeley, even though it's months and months away. At least we had a good couple of months together, and she and I will at least try to stay friends. I'll see how that goes."

I'd been over this with Sara already. I guess she was hoping that Caroline had changed her mind and was going to stick it out with me. I wish Caroline had changed her mind, too. I was game for a long-distance romance. In an earlier time, rejection like this would have broken me. Now, it's just part of life. Good things happen, bad things happen, but life just goes on.

"I think she's making a mistake," Sara reassured me.

"Well, I know she is," I agreed. "She doesn't think so, though. Trevor even yelled at her. But what are you going to do?"

"Keep you for myself?"

We both stood up, still holding on to each other.

It was going to be a good year. Finish school, then spend more than half the summer in New York City before classes start up at Pratt.

And a wide, wide horizon ahead of me.

"We should get going," Sara said. "Your parents want to take us out to dinner, remember?"

It was getting late, the lights aimed at the tombstone flooded the glass with brightness. In the matter of an hour, a single dim glow would stand out in the dark cemetery, just one of the ways I'd thought of to show that *I* had cared too, and still did.

CHAPTER 11

A letter unsent but well meant

Dear William,

I would hope that this letter finds you well, but since you are dead I can't know. Part of me hopes that there is something beyond what we have here and now, and that you see the world from where you are. If not, then at least I can get all this off my chest. I thought it might be a good idea to write out how I feel.

I imagine myself talking to you as I write, actually getting in a word edgewise, finally able to interrupt your nonstop talking. Finally able to say all the things I wanted to say but never got a chance to tell you. You would never shut up. Wish I could hear you now, but it still doesn't mean that you never did shut up.

We didn't get along, you and I. I didn't think that the world suddenly changed things between us when you died. I didn't think you were some kind of saint. I didn't gloss over the things you did wrong. Maybe it was because I was so detached from things, so isolated, that I didn't have this big hole in my life when you died. Or maybe I did, and took out all my anger on the world. With you gone, I couldn't keep on making excuses about why Dad and Mom paid so little attention to me.

I had to stand up and make a mark. I couldn't keep on blaming you for stuff. Yeah, Dad and Mom did get along better with you. But that's just how it was. Doesn't mean they didn't like me, or that they hated me, which in my screwed-up mind I sometimes imagined. It just means that some people get along better, and some don't. I wish it wasn't like that. I wish things could have been better between us, at least.

I never thought for a moment that you cared about me. Everyone insisted that you did, that you loved me, that you were this wonderful person. I never believed it because all I saw was Dad and Mom going out of their way to make your life better. Meanwhile, it seemed to me that they felt I didn't need so much, so I was left to fall by the wayside.

They could see that I didn't need as much from them as you, so they gave you what you needed. I should have told them that I needed more from them too.

But the thing is, deep down, I knew that you needed a lot of help; and all because some doctor screwed up delivering you. That wasn't your fault. I know that I had lots of decent breaks in life, just because I was born healthy. I should have been more understanding. I see that now. But I was just a kid.

Still, even with the screwed-up birth and people making fun of you, you still made something of yourself. You did better than lots of people who are perfectly healthy. You made more of a difference to the people you met than most of the smart kids, the school team players and the in-crowds. You made people forget all the bad things about you once they came to know you. And they forgave your faults. That shows how much you came to mean to them.

For some reason, I couldn't forgive you. It seemed that I did all the right things and still ended up being compared to you. And I never seemed to come out of those comparisons well. I hated it, hated that I couldn't stand out no matter what I did. I'd get great grades but it was just expected of me. You stood out simply by beating the odds.

I never thought you cared. I keep coming back to that, but it's something that I know molded my personality. If you're still floating around, as it were, you probably got a kick out of watching me throw up when Buzz showed me the trust fund. A last laugh for you, proving me wrong after all this time. I thought you didn't give a damn about me. I'd *just thought it was you, Dad, and Mom as one big family, while I was the odd one out. I'd always thought that you were shutting me out, pushing me aside, all of you.*

And then I find out you cared about me more than you could have ever explained. You were never good with words. I figure that Buzz helped you write half your papers at college—although maybe that's being uncharitable. You weren't too good with actions, either. I mean, Christmas... that last Christmas you were here, you had nothing good to say about anything I did. Was it simply me being good at what I did that got you so mad that you had to lash out at me?

I don't know... maybe I just saw it that way and didn't listen. Maybe we both should take some blame for that.

All I know is that you made up for it big time. You took nearly everything you had and made it mine, and all to make up for all the stuff you thought I'd lost out on. The money they spent on your medical bills, on your schooling, on everything... I didn't ask for it and it wasn't given. It goes both ways. Maybe I could have pushed more, maybe I could have tried to be more a part of the family with everyone. Maybe I could have tried to remember more of the good stuff instead of focusing on all the bad things.

I can't really say that I loved you, Will. You were my brother, and it bothers me that you got a raw deal out of life. But I can't say that I loved you. I just didn't feel that connection to you. I didn't hate you though, and I genuinely wish that things could have been different for you. I wish we could have been brothers like my friend Trevor and his brother. But we weren't. We were just Andrew and William Simmons, always butting heads, always arguing.

It really is a shame that it took your dying for me finally to be part of the family. For a while, I thought that with you gone, I was going to be the only brother left. But it turned out that I was still going to have to compete with your memory, your ghost. Some day, I would even be the older brother. I'd be twenty-four years old and getting older, *while you didn't age a day. Forever twenty-four and always Dad and Mom's beautiful boy while I continued to age.*

But in my heart, you are always going to be my older brother, even though you don't age a day. I'm going to take what you gave me and make the best of it. You showed your true feelings by taking a big part of what belonged to you and giving it to me when you didn't have to. Now, it's my turn to do the same. You have a nice tombstone now, and I'm going to see about setting up a scholarship in your name. I'm sure I'll think of other things, or Buzz and Sara and other people will give me ideas.

At the very least, I can find ways to show how much I care about you and what you've done for me.

Take care, my only brother, wherever you may be...

Andrew

Breaking Dawn
DONNA SHELTON
Is friendship forever? Secrets, betrayal, remorse and suicide

The Finer Points of Becoming Machine
EMILY ANDREWS
Emily is a mess, like her suicide attempt

Marty's Diary
FRANCES CROSS
How to handle stepparents

The Only Brother
CAIAS WARD
Sibling rivalry doesn't end at the grave

Seeing Red
PETER LANCETT
The pain and the pleasure of self-harm

SADDLEBACK
EDUCATIONAL PUBLISHING